Dominated by deadly, visceral action, betrayals within betrayals, and a bloody pursuit across a vast alien moon Agranoff's *Goddamn Killing Machines* echoes science fiction's Golden Age and the innate suspense, technological detail, and reality-building that were its hallmarks. That said, this is a modern novel, one in which Agranoff's own driving socio-political concerns come to the fore as he details our far- and even-farther-futures, environmental horrorshows in which humanity seems at odds with every living thing it comes in contact with, including itself."

- KURT BAUMEISTER, AUTHOR OF *PAX AMERICANA*

GODDAMN KILLING MACHINES

DAVID AGRANOFF

CL◢SH

This one is for my father. When I was young I saw many hours of him at his desk writing. It meant a great deal to me to see those hours turn into books on the shelf. Not to forget all the support he showed me even when I was being a dumbass.

CHAPTER 1

IT WAS easy for Spacers to forget what a wasteland Earth had become. It had been five years since he had seen it from orbit. The birthplace of humanity reduced to an eyesore out the window of the orbital jumper. He didn't feel much about it. It was a professional skill, the ability to witness the most fucked up things life had to offer and tuck it away.

Nick Jarvis was a soldier of fortune, a killer, and a war criminal. Despite being Earth-born he hated being dirt-side, and spent the last two years struggling to get back to space. This was not how he planned it.

The hand-cuffs were tight and the shackles on his feet were heavy despite the slightly-less-than-Earth artificial gravity. He had grown used to a heavy feeling on Earth, but never the heat or the grime. The sweat and the toil was how human life was meant to be lived; as a solider he was trained to handle any environment, but the control of extra-terrain existence had become like the comfort of home.

He moved towards the window and took in the sight. The orbiter rocketed silently two-hundred miles above North America. He could see Toronto rising in the distance, the skyline visible. The shimmer of the Anti-Grav lift was in the beginning stages of lifting the city away from the hostile surface.

As they passed the Rocky Mountains, Jarvis knew they would pass over Sammy soon. As irrational as it was he put his hands on the glass. He prayed for his son, feeling only the slight cold of the vacuum. He believed in his heart Melissa would keep his son safe.

Outside the window above the curve of the planet he saw the UN Earth Command Center growing from a dot. The massive size of the city, was visible from the ground. It had been in stationary orbit above the headquarters in New York City but now the city that never sleeps was heading toward a couple centuries of eternal night, it was in motion. Spinning slow enough to maintain gravity and constantly launching Jumpers. The second exodus was in full swing and Earth was like a room with a light flicked on. The roaches were in flight.

The end of a rifle poked him in the back. Jarvis turned to see a fresh cut teenager in a UN Space-Corps uniform.

"Let's go, get ready to dock." The young soldier tried to sound hard; he failed. Jarvis assumed he didn't need to tell this kid who he was. The sweat on his brow and the very slight shaking of his rifle said he knew. Jarvis considered letting it go but decided it was good to set the tone.

"You poke me again Junior, you'll eat that fuckin' rifle."

"I know who you are."

Jarvis looked him up and down. "I can tell."

The young soldier nodded. "I helped arrest your whole team."

"You look pretty healthy, considering."

The soldier laughed. "Why didn't you fight? The others fought."

"Who's here?"

The soldier shook his head. "Why didn't you fight?"

He didn't have anything to prove to this kid, who was probably born off-world and probably never took a breath of Earth air. He had enough scars on his arms and one signature scar by his right eye. No one would mistake Nick Jarvis for a candy-ass. The reality was that the most livable places left on Earth were the cities that existed miles above the surface. The air was thinner and colder, thus more livable than the heat and humidity the under cities dealt with. Nine cities were chosen by the UN to escape. In a feat of twenty-third century engineering beyond his ability to understand, the cities were rising using Anti-Grav lifts. Inching into orbit. At the same time, domes were being built to encase the atmosphere; the oxygen supplied by the swamps and canals that replaced most of the streets.

London, NYC, Chicago, Paris, Toronto, Vancouver, Istanbul, Buenos Aires, and Nairobi were chosen as colony-cities. The locals called them Jump Cities; they had become the next generation of ark ships and were functional eco-systems on their own. The citizens who launched would not live to land on Hermea, the target world, but their children's children would live one day in the same city under a new sun.

It was better than the first ark-ships currently crossing the void to humanity's new home eight light years away at Sirius A. Those ships were coffin movers packed into every inch with seeds, 3D printers, and hypersleep chambers. At three percent the speed of light, the First Wavers would sleep for two-hundred and eighty-seven years before starting their new lives from scratch.

His species had turned their home world into a dump. Not worth the investment to fix. The discovery of fresh worlds and building of ark ships had made humanity's birthplace an unwise investment. Three options remained: struggling to survive in the colonies in the solar system, two hundred plus years as an ice cube, or city life.

He didn't fight his arrest because staying on Earth was no longer an option. He had not planned on having a family. He tried to talk Melissa out of having Sammy, but Earth pregnancies were becoming more rare with each year. She wanted desperately to have him, and now that he was born Nick Jarvis loved his son more deeply than he thought possible.

He had promised her he would find away to get them on to one of the Jump Cities. He knew Cooper was the reason he was here.. He knew there was deal to be made. The UN could put them on trial but a lot of the dirty deeds were paid for by off-planet accounts overseen by member governments.

Jarvis dragged his chains back to the airlock door and stared out the small window. The docking bay opened and waited for their approach. The sounds of docking rumbled through the small orbiter. Jarvis tried to calm himself. He despised Cooper, a bureaucrat who spent his life smoothing operations between the United Nations and corporations who generally worked all sides of conflicts through-out the solar system.

"Docking complete," the station announced before it interfaced with Jarvis and uploaded the station's rules and protocols. The air lock spun open and the young solider walked through first. They felt the rush of fresher air. His chains and feet felt suddenly heavier as Jarvis walked into the command station. They had Earth-like gravity.

Half a dozen armed soldiers waited for them. Jarvis suppressed an urge to say "boo." Each one of them knew who he was. The fresh cut waited inside the orbiter with Jarvis for his escorts to lead him out of the hangar bay. A crowd had gathered at the second level to get a peek. Not a single person smiled, but he didn't expect applause. He never wanted to be famous; as a mercenary you wanted nothing more than to be infamous. He looked up and tried to match the stares of as many as he could. He felt shame for nothing.

He saw the military-style jumper that was being loaded for a mission. They were preparing for something intimate, something they didn't trust drones to do. His specialty.

A pair of doors opened and Jarvis walked into the command center alone. Computer stations and drone jockeys wore headsets, barked out commands, and interfaced in VR. Screens floated in front of pilots connected to drones on battlefields below. They didn't notice him. Jarvis had been in this type of command center before. The drone jockeys were here in body but anything amounting to soul was down below; the VR tricked the mind so completely it wasn't uncommon for heart attacks to happen when the drones took fire.

Earth was a conflict zone, the under cities still raged over dirt that caused strife for a thousand years. Palestine, Argentina, Iceland, Alaska, or the Yukon. The trouble spots had been his home away from home for many years. There was a passion for land wherever humanity planted its various flags. No matter how dry and dead, there was no collection of dirt that brought out the fighting spirit like Earth. Life on Mars was a struggle and you couldn't survive without horse-sized radiation pills, but most of it was well policed. The habitat rings in Earth's orbit were more than a police state; they were Big Brother. Everyone focused on protecting the Exodus. The moons of Saturn and Jupiter were not the Wild West they used to be. Ark ship construction was big business out on the moons, until some woman figured out the math to lift cities. Life in the outer solar system was bleak.

The door shut behind him. Cooper sat in the command chair and didn't seem to notice that he had entered the room. Jarvis looked over his shoulder at the massive holo-screen lowered into front of the chair. It resembled a bug's eye view divided into a dozen live pictures. Around the earth drones floated high enough to not be noticed, but close enough to get images. He recognized conflicts he had fought in, the standard Chinese script flashing on the digital signs around the Santiago markets, the caravans of horses pulling cars across the cracked highways of the American dunes. His eyes scanned all these things but stopped on a feed from San Francisco. He was surprised how clean and functional the city remained. He understood that it had been built up into the sky decades ago.

"A lot of planning went into this day," Cooper turned the

command chair around to face him. "Colonel Nick Jarvis. How long has it been?"

"Not long enough."

"Mars, ten years ago?"

It had been seven years, but Jarvis wasn't playing the game. "What am I doing here?"

"I have to thank you for walking in on your own."

Jarvis held up his handcuffs.

Cooper nodded. "Well you must understand the rest of your squad were not as accommodating."

"How many has she killed so far?" Jarvis nodded at the screen.

Cooper was not amused. "You think this is funny, Colonel?"

"No, I don't." Jarvis smiled. "I was waiting for you to give me the reason why I shouldn't just kill everyone on this station."

Now Cooper smiled. "You and I both know two very good reasons are down there on Earth. Not to mention the war crimes you and your team are wanted for across the solar system. I have Martian prosecutors that are dying to put you on trial."

"Garay is dead; Eden killed him."

"Maybe, but you were his commander and his death doesn't get you off the hook. I need the whole team and then we will talk."

"You want me to bring in Eden."

Cooper blinked one eye to control his server menu. The handcuffs disappeared into a vapor. Jarvis's wrists still felt sore and slowly his feet came free. It took every bit of self-control he had not reach out and strangle Cooper. Cooper motioned Jarvis to follow him.

"I need to know that Melissa and Sammy are safe."

"You are in no position to make demands."

Jarvis looked around the command center, UN Materials, with corporation funding. This was an expensive operation. Nothing had this kind of money anymore except the ark missions and Jump-cities. Paris had just entered orbit and in a few months New York would follow. It wouldn't be long before

Earth was in their rear-view mirror. He had to play along. He could get the squad pardons and one-way tickets.

A drone flew into the room and carried a package past Jarvis. His jaw dropped; he thought it had been destroyed with his ship. The metal case was locked and programmed to open only for his retinal scan.

"You shouldn't have."

Cooper shrugged. "A gift and a sign of trust."

The laser reached up to his eyes and the locks snapped open. He took the case and the drone flew away. His smile was genuine. The smart pistols he now held were one of kind, hand-made for him, gold plated 9mm pistols linked to his DNA. No one else in the universe could hold them. They gave an electric shock to anyone unrecognizable who picked them up and they had self-replicating clips. He held them in his hands and felt the pinprick of the computer scanning and identifying him.

Jarvis spun the pistols and pushed them into his belt. He looked up to see if Cooper was watching him. When Cooper's eyes were elsewhere, Jarvis lifted the velvet lining of the case to see if it was where he left it. He glanced quickly and saw Eden's face. A picture he had taken of her; he didn't want her or anyone else to know he had it. The retro photo was printed on glossy paper like they did in the twentieth century; it was Eden, on a beach. It looked like an engineered one, the kind popular beside lakes on Mars or the Europa colonies. He had been drunk, so he didn't remember where on Mars it was taken. The fake sun hung low in the sky and backlit her body. Wearing a two piece bikini and a smile, her arms spread out wide as if saying, *look at me.*

Years ago he hid the photo in his pistol case. He was relieved that it was still there. Still, he didn't want anyone else to see it. He closed the case with a snap. .

"You are all that's left. You bring her in and then you'll have your answers."

Cooper grinned. "She just arrived. Martian authorities were

not eager to engage her in combat, and we promised if they let her slip off-world she would never be allowed back."

"I thought she was gone, really gone."

Jarvis looked over his shoulder at the massive holoscreen as it lowered in front of Cooper's chair. Resembling a bug's eye, the view was divided into a dozen live pictures. Around Earth, drones floated high enough to not be noticed, but close enough to get images. He recognized conflicts he had fought in, the standard Chinese script flashing on the digital signs around Santiago markets, the caravans of horses pulling cars across cracked highways of the American dunes. His eyes scanned all these but stopped on a feed from San Francisco. He was surprised how clean and functional the city remained. He understood it had been built up into the sky decades ago. The 110th floor of more than one building was street level in the new San Fran.

The city street was crowded, and the evening foot traffic to citizens to bars and restaurants. Jarvis didn't have to study the image long before he found her. It wasn't hard to find the woman who had broken his heart. She blamed him for the heartbreak, he felt the wounds opening. Amanda Eden walked along a street in a formal dress. Her hair was shorter, just over her shoulder, but still slightly curled. The dress clung to her figure as it always had: perfectly. Her eyes, hazel and glowing they twinkled like Venus before dawn.

Jarvis battled with his emotions in the moment. Relief that she was alive and free. Warmth at the sight of her. Anger that she had come back to Earth, and worst, the knowledge that he was going to have to bring her in. There was no doubt in his mind that Cooper had tried and failed. He knew his mission now.

CHAPTER 2

AMANDA EDEN never liked the smell of Earth. The people born here, or who grew up here, couldn't smell it, but she did. She felt the dirty air inflating her lungs and hacked on her first Earth breathes like a cat with a hairball. She adjusted as the day wore on. She straightened her dress and walked through the crowd. She had been on the Vomit Comet from Mars long enough to feel the effects of zero G and her legs felt a little wobbly. It was also her first time alone in months.

She never wanted to come here, but hoped it was the last place the authorities looked for her. The low clouds hung around near the floor of the platform. She saw the lights from the islands off the coast. That was where she wanted to go, but a taxi to the closest island would have cleared her credits out.

She had just forty-two credits, enough for a tram ticket and a place to stay if she could find a roach motel with a flashing vacancy sign. She got off at the Haight Street stop at the edge of upper Golden Gate Park. The platform had open slats where the tops of trees poked through. Crowds walked on the clear glass where the paths had once been and looked down into the jungle that the Under-Golden Gate Park had become.

This was one of the few cities in North America that still

functioned. The under-city had rewilded but that didn't mean people were not down there.

Her mother had spent a lot of time here, told her all about her youth in this city. It was a time when everyone built toward the sky. Eden never listened closely. She hated her mother, and everything she had forced her to do.

She connected to the city's data-stream, and found the neighborhood server. She scanned until she found the visitor-user interface. A list of popular restaurants, clubs, and motels appeared in her vision. The cheapest room was going to cost her sixty credits. She could have afforded it if she had not bought a locker back at the spaceport to stash her duffel and coat. She had looked briefly in the small mirror inside the locker. Her dress was an elegant red, open-backed and tied around her neck and hung just above her thighs..

Amanda Eden was thirty-four years old and thanks to missions that required hypersleep travel, she didn't look a day over twenty-five. Her body was a marvel of science and nature. Jarvis admitted to everyone that he picked her because of her perfect figure, sparkling hazel eyes, and charming smile. Every team needed women; why not a woman who was easy on the eyes and who could manipulate men? She wasn't proud of it but the reality was that exploiting men was part of Eden's skill set.

The UN gave her the best bio-technological upgrades known to science and then fight training and weapons were a simple download. Strength and skill didn't need to be natural talent.

She was an elite gymnast in high school, fourth in all-solar system tournament—close enough to smell the gold medal. She naturally possessed intelligence, strength, and beauty. She was perfect. After ten years of combat she had managed to only lose one hand, which was easily replaced by a new, stronger vat-grown hand. She had a brutal right hook and a few scars—the worst of which were hidden under her curly dirty blond hair.

She walked back to the park and stood in the middle of the crowd. She looked back for her partner and relaxed when she didn't see him. The people walked past her on their way to bars and nightclubs. It was that time of night in the city. A man walked toward her with a pit bull trotting behind him. He was lily white and had green dreadlocks tied back and tucked under a visor. Eden slid to block his path. He smiled a grill full of gold teeth, one of which glowed, swirling different colors like a lava lamp. He shook a vial of liquid at her.

"Hey there beautiful, you looking for some Dragon Breath?"

She was looking for credits, not a high, but she had pretty good idea the guy selling Dragon Breath on the street wasn't rolling in credits. It was the cheaper more prolific of Vapes, the designer drug that was all-chemical but also interacted with the net-jack most people connected to the data stream with. It was a high and a wetware trip at the same time. It gave the feeling of floating on a living data stream.

"I am, but I don't want that little thing." She tipped her head, playing coy and sexy.

"Oh I got big ones, sweetheart." He leered at her.

"You men always think you do. I don't need a man, I need *the* man." She arched one brow.

The dealer took off his sunglasses and she saw that his eyes were augmented so far beyond natural that they looked like headlights jacked from a Jeep.

"Maybe I *am* the man."

Eden playfully giggled, and wagged her finger.

"I don't think so. *The* man doesn't shuck wetware hacks on the corner." Eden turned and walked a few steps giving those mechanical eyes a good two seconds to focus in on her backside. She stopped, gave her hips a wiggle, and looked back. "Why don't you take me to the man? The *real* man."

The dealer shook his head.

"I think he'll want to see me," she cajoled.

The dealer looked her up and down before put the vial back in his pocket and motioning her to follow.

The man ended up being an Israeli gangster name Danny Stein; his enemies called him Danny the Hebe. His parents called him Daniel Steinhoff, but they hadn't seen him in twenty years. They were asleep for the next two hundred and eighty-seven years. They were UN Officials working for the Holy Land who got tickets as soon as Tel Aviv was not chosen to become a colony. Danny was offered a pod but the big sleep didn't appeal to him. He owned clubs in Dubai, Lebanon, and along the US west coast. The world was ending and he provided much needed escape. He had a London apartment, likely where he would move when Earth was finally dead.

Eden was disgusted after reading the file she found on Steinhoff, but the dealer had found the perfect mark. An organized criminal with lots of money and one she didn't mind putting an end to..

The club was called The Titan Ballroom. The dealer was not allowed inside. He was still debating with the front door bouncers as two mountain-sized thugs grabbed her arm and, she thought about breaking his arm as he lead her through the crowd. It parted for them and many club-goers stared at Eden. At the back of the room, naked men and women circled golden poles while the crowd cheered and transferred credits.

The music was so loud it rattled her bones; she tried not to let it overwhelm her. Jarvis taught her to scan rooms, look for threats, plan escapes. With the dancing lights and the ear-thumping music it was impossible. She followed the thugs through the kaleidoscope of flesh and vapors and tried not to breathe too deeply. The smell of sweat and drugs hung like a cloud. Eden was tempted to pull out her knife and see if she could cut out a piece of it.

The first thug stopped and turned to stand in front of a door in the back. He shifted slightly and Eden saw where his pistol was holstered under his coat. She smiled at the other huge man; they looked identical. Same ugly, slick-backed long hair and black jacket. The second thug's jacket had a bulge in the same spot. She assumed they were illegally vat-grown bodyguards from Io. They looked scary but she could tell they were slow.

The door opened to an overweight man behind a desk. He wore a vintage suit and tie. He held what looked like an Argentine cigar and behind him stood a nervous-looking woman in a tin swatch of fabric that could barely be called a dress. Her perfectly curled long blond hair dropped over one shoulder and she stood still, like a living statue. The man tipped his head, but Eden noticed a camera close to the ceiling that moved with him. He wasn't actually here, she realized. What she was looking at was a very expensive hologram sent through the data-stream from somewhere far away. Nonetheless, Eden smelled the cigar; if she slapped him she was sure they would both feel something very close to reality. She found these holographic transmissions spooky.

Danny Stein smiled and licked his lips. "I told my boys that we didn't need any more dancers or whores but they insisted I have a look."

His accent was Middle Eastern. The thugs moved to each side of her, close enough she could smell the slight musk of cheap vape on them. Eden shook her head.

"I'm not a whore and I'm not interested in dancing." Eden's voice was firm.

Danny looked at the thug on Eden's right. He raised an eyebrow. He looked back at her. "What do you want then?"

"A different kind of job. Enforcer, assassin. Whatever you need." She waited while they laughed.

Stein cleared his throat. "Sweetheart, I got a very high-paid army that works my clubs." He gestured at the two thugs.

Eden smiled. *He was asking for it*, she thought to herself and touched her thumb to her index finger.

CHAPTER 3

THE SUB-ORBITAL JUMPER skipped over the upper atmosphere like a stone thrown across a stream. Cooper settled in for the ride. The jumper dropped into the atmosphere, just above the Texas border and made its way across the sky towards the San Fran platform. He sat in the rear with a group of fresh-faced Marines. A few UN officials and marshals sat up front, acting as if they were in charge.

Jarvis put the command node into his left ear to boost his signal. This gave Cooper and command up top a bird's eye view of what he saw as well as every vital sign in his body.

Jarvis flipped on a screen that tracked Eden.

Cooper, are you there? He transmitted the question through a neural link.

I'm here, Colonel.

Jarvis spun around the screen that showed the drone feed.

We lost her while we were in the Ionosphere.

The signal changed to the inside of a dance club. This security footage was ripped off the grid; in most post-American cities the UN had overridden the local feeds. The camera zoomed to the back of the club. Two unnaturally large men were escorting Eden through a crowd. One of the men parted the crowd while the other kept a firm grip on her arm. Jarvis was surprised the man's hand still functioned.

He knew she was up to something. Music in the club was bass heavy and played loud enough in the jumper to get the attention of the waiting soldiers. Half a dozen soldiers sat strapped in. They watched Jarvis, who didn't seem bothered by the ship's shaking as they re-entered Earth's atmosphere. The team they put together were Marine recon units with Earth-based combat experience, although most were born and raised in the habitat ring. Being an Earth-born Marine meant nothing to these men but it was something special to Jarvis. Most of his team had been born on Earth; he felt it gave them an edge, a harder edge. It made them more human.

One of the young soldiers tapped Jarvis on the shoulder.

"Club is owned by an Israeli gangster; security is all ex-IDF and Mossad. Mean fuckers with top-shelf training."

"Poor bastards." Jarvis laughed. His humor faded when the sound of automatic weapons blasted from the video feed. He spun the imagine control around to the front door. His jaw dropped. It was sight of a ghost. Jamal Garay had the front door security in front of him on his knees. He was using the guard's own rifle to choke him. His partner was struggling on the floor.

You said he was dead. Cooper's tone conveyed fear.

Shit. He was nearly speechless. His biggest monster; the only human Jarvis feared. He was supposed to be dead. Eden told him she had killed him. Left him buried on Mars.

Garay threw away the rifle and grabbed a shock baton in his right hand and a pistol in his left. A third guard rushed him from his left. The single shot he fired took the man's head up and sent chunks of skull and brain all over the people sitting at the table inside the door. Screams drowned out the music as Garay slammed the baton into another table, sending patrons screaming.

Jarvis looked around the jumper at the young soldiers. They didn't stand a chance against Eden now he knew they would die if they got close to Garay.

Eden knew this was coming but after years of restraining him, and keeping Garay's aggression in check, she was still shocked at the unleashed fury.

The guard holding her let go. He and his partner rushed towards Garay. Eden looked up to make sure the security cameras were catching this for Stein to watch.

The crowd screamed and headed for the exit. Garay followed the flow, using the club manaager as a human shield. The security guards lost him in the mix. Eden watched the guards spin slowly holding their pistols high. Garay burst through the crowd and pushed a dancer to the floor. He swung his shock baton at full force against the guard's kneecap. The man fell on his remaining knee. Garay ducked behind him in time to use the man to absorb two bullets. The body shook violently as the bullets sliced through the armor.

Garay put his pistol to the back of his now-dead shield's neck. He used his thumb to switch the mode to canon. A roar echoed through the club as the bullet rushed through the first guard's neck and slammed into the armor of the second, knocking that guard back. If He wasn't dead but he wouldn't stand again. His ribs had shattered under the armor.

The club was clear now except for Eden, Garay, and the dying. Garay stood up, his black skin covered in blood. Garay's calm was unnerving. So far their plan was working.

"Stein? You listening?" Garay paused and took a few deep breaths. "I'm taking every dime."

Eden stared; it was not hard to act intimidated. "Don't kill me please, I'll do anything you want."

"Don't move." He pointed at her.

Stein's voice echoed through the club. "You just killed a very expensive security guard."

Garay shook his head and walked to the bar. He jumped over and fished through the pockets of the manager. Holding up the manger's bank pad, he opened the dead man's eyes to unlock it with his retinal ID. Garay knew he had only one shot at this, as within minutes of death the retinal scan would no longer work. The pad was linked to the cash register, and within minutes they would have the night's earnings. This interface linked in minutes to all Stein's accounts. They could get them briefly but any money transferred into his account would have tracers added. The money was not the point. Garay could keep the money. She didn't want it; she only wanted the job.

"Wait!" The voice from the speaker sounded less than confident. "You have no idea who you are fucking with."

Eden knew Stein had forgotten about her. She leaned down and worked dead fingers off the guard's pistol. She lifted and pointed the weapon, shooting out the whiskey bottle that sat inches from Garay's head.

He ducked behind the bar. They had to make this look good. She ran into a slide on the floor and fired at Garay as soon as he was back in sight. He returned fire but she had knocked a table down to take the bullet. The table split into plastic bits around her.

She jumped up on the bar and ran its length. Reaching the end, she jumped down and kicked Garay's pistol to the floor. She gripped him around the neck with her rebuilt arm. He was three times her size but struggled to breathe. In his hand, she could watch the transfer on the bank pad's screen. The night's profit was uploading to their ghost account. When it finished with tonight's money, it would initialize with all connected accounts. If they got one dime out of the primary accounts they could be traced.

Transfer was at 96%

Eden released her grip slightly.

It ticked up to 97%.

She and Garay share a quick glace she hoped no one else saw.

Out of the corner of her eye she saw the transfer reach 98%.

The plan was working but her timing had to be perfect. She had to come out the hero.

She whispered as softly as she could into Garay's ear, "Are you ready?"

Finally, the bank transfer glowed, *One hundred percent.* Next, a line flashed: connecting to primary accounts. They only had seconds.

She gave Garay a squeeze for the camera; a normal person would have been choked out by now. The pressure was enough to make Garay drop the bank pad. Eden kicked it away. She loosened her grip on him to point her pistol and shot the bank pad. It exploded into pieces.

"No!" Garay yelled as he pushed Eden back. She slammed into the bar. Garay ran for the front door. They fired at each other, missing by inches. Eden felt shards of the floor spit up into her ankles.

Garay was out of the club into the street. Now she was alone with the corpses. Hard to believe, but it worked. The lights in the club slowly brightened.

A round drone the size of a baseball floated high in the room. It spun and released light that formed a hologram. From the right angles, it appeared as if Danny Stein was in the room. "Wow, baby girl, you are something else." He whistled. "You say you want a job, but I've been looking for a new mistress." It came out like a question.

Eden dropped the heavy pistol on the bar. "Baby girl? Are you serious?" She grabbed a glass and a bottle of something expensive. She poured herself a shot and took a swig. "I just saved you a lot money, not to mention the cash you've been wasting to feed those useless vat-grown guards."

"So what do you want?"

"I need to be on Earth until the exodus, and I have no interest in sweating it out dirt-side. I need a job that will get me quietly on to one of the jump-cities."

She didn't want to seem desperate. She could've just stolen the money but this was about getting citizenship and ticket to escape when the time came. Garay played along because all he wanted was money. Staying on earth was a death sentence they both knew it, and in that sense he had the leverage.

"Being my lady gets you an apartment in London and a one way ticket to a new world."

"So does being your bodyguard, with less expectations. Everyone will think I'm one of your girls. The perfect front; it won't look like you have a bodyguard. I am trained in various forms of combat and augmented off the books."

Danny nodded. "You're easier on the eyes than those vat-monkeys."

"And unlike them, I can protect you."

Danny smiled. "You're hired."

CHAPTER 4

JARVIS THOUGHT they sold it pretty well. The soldiers watching the screen over his shoulder seemed to believe that Eden and Garay were actually fighting. He reached up and tapped his screen, spinning through options to find the outside feed. He got multiple views of the streets around the city. He knew Cooper's drone jockeys were scanning every face in the crowd.

"You won't find him," Jarvis said over the open-voice channel to Cooper and then looked at the Marines. "He won't find him. Garay will be using a face scrambler to avoid the gangster."

"That was Jamal Garay." The oldest-looking Marine didn't hide his shock.

We need to abort. Jarvis commented through the private link to Cooper.

Negative, we may never get another chance.

Jarvis didn't want to say this. *I'm not sure I can take him down.*

You trained him.

Jarvis ignored that. He could have told him to stock up on body bags, or some other smart-ass remark, but thought it best for Cooper to deal with the consequences.

Jarvis looked out the window. San Francisco appeared below as if floating on clouds. The lights from the skyline were a beacon pulling them closer. The Marines were unpacking their drones. Jarvis unboxed the one given to him. It was a sleek black machine.

"Nice drone," he told the one nearest him.

It was a standard issue UN Security Forces robotic drone, designed to work independently with its own AI or under direct interface control. Each one was personally coded to the soldier's neural net, and was impossible to hack—AI was programmed to be loyal—imprinted like a dog to its person. Rangers called them man's best friend for a reason. Even with a thumbnail-sized nuclear reactor, a .45 caliber automatic rifle built in, and self-replicating bullets, they were still small and light enough to hold. They were the most important weapons in modern warfare.

Jarvis unfolded the drone's wings. He used his interface to turn it on. The oldest Marine, Anderson according to his uniform, sat across from Jarvis.

"What happened down there?" Anderson asked.

"It was a scam, Garay wasn't trying to fight her," Jarvis told him.

"That was not trying?" Anderson shook his head.

Jarvis shook his head. "Not one bit; she was gaining the mark's confidence."

The Marine connected a gun to his drone. "Why does she want to work for Danny the Hebe?"

"She's a fugitive. Needs work off the books. Who better to work for?" Jarvis laughed.

"Even on Earth you can't just kill people like that," Another Marine, Lambo, chimed in.

Jarvis gave him the 'who the fuck are you' look.

Anderson let go of his drone, which floated in front of him with a low buzz. "You upload the file on these bastards, Lambo?"

"No way he read it," said a third Marine. "He's too calm."

"You know what they call these fucking psychos?"Asked Lambo.

Cooper's hologram materialized in the cockpit. "Look alive, everyone."

Jarvis never got a chance to roll his eyes. He didn't need to hear his history repeated. The jumper bounced around in and out of traffic flying above the city. Jarvis looked at the hologram out of habit, even if the real Cooper was a hundred miles above them in orbit.

"I can't talk you into ending this mission? You wrote most of that report. I shouldn't have to explain to how things have changed with Garay in the mix." Jarvis said as he used a cloth to shine one of his pistols.

"Our whole team is very impressed." Cooper waved his hands at the interplanetary agents and marshals sitting beyond the Marines. Jarvis nodded.

"Is that so? Jamal Garay isn't just a soldier. He might as well be an entire army. Insurgency after insurgency has made him into one nasty motherfucker," Jarvis told them.

"And therein lies the problem, Colonel Jarvis, if your mercenaries—" Cooper began.

"Contractors." Jarvis interrupted him.

"Whatever. I know it's nasty down there. The rules are, shall we say, gray; but if you had followed a higher code of conduct off-world we wouldn't be in this position would we?" Cooper sounded exasperated.

Jarvis slid the top of his pistol back and snapped the first bullet into the chamber. "Just don't expect them to stay on the platform."

One of the marshals stepped out of the pilot's cabin. "We lost Garay."

A couple of the Marines relaxed involuntarily.

Jarvis nodded. "We grab Eden, he'll find us."

The ship twisted between glass buildings, flying in silent mode. They were swarmed by spider-drones. Jarvis looked up and followed the sound of the crawling drones. The pilot energized the hull and dead drones fell away. The ship angled between buildings and came up next to the target tower. Jarvis looked at the troops Cooper had given him and wondered if they had parents or if they were vat-grown. Not that it mattered; they signed up to be here, and they would make great drone bait.

Jarvis controlled the camera with his thumb and found Eden walking down the crowded street. She looked up every few seconds. He could see that she was worried. Confusion at being this close to her raced through him. He had tried so hard to put her out of his mind. He loved Melissa and the pain of being away from Sammy was like a vise twisting his insides, but seeing Eden again moved something in him.

Under the watchful eye of Jarvis's drone, Eden walked down Haight Street. Jarvis felt like a creep, watching her without her knowledge. He linked his drone footage to the jumper command center and they weaved between buildings until they reached the park's perimeter. Everyone watched his feed on their visors, which hung off their helmets.

Jarvis concentrated on the sensors and signals coming in from the drone. Eden stopped walking and her heart rate rose. She didn't move.

"She knows," Jarvis uttered.

"That's impossible," A marshal said behind Jarvis.

Eden jumped into the street, nearly cutting off a bicyclist and running in front of an air taxi about to take off. It was a move designed to lose someone at street level. Jarvis didn't buy it; she would assume that she was being watched by a drone. She was heading for a crowded place.

"Release your bogies," the Commander yelled to his men.

The back hatch to the jumper opened and let in a huge gust of cold air. One by one the Marines stepped to the edge and released their drones.

Jarvis dialed up the city's net and found the address and interface for the club she had run into. The drone had lost her image as she ducked into the club a few moments earlier. Jarvis turned around and ran to the back of the jumper. He slapped the button, opening the back hatch wider.

"Get me as close to the club as you can," he ordered the Marine.

Jarvis directed the drone to dip down toward the club. The jumper flew down toward the roof of the club, a four-story building with a fire escape in back. With the back hatch to the jumper open, the strong winds of their high altitude rushed around the inside of the jumper. Jarvis jumped out the back.

He landed with a thud on the metal fire escape stairs.

His drone flew toward the club; the camera sent an image of the door opening and a goth woman flashing her ID. Jarvis increased its speed and the drone whizzed through the door. The woman and the front door bouncer both turned as they felt the wind rush past. The drone camouflaged itself to blend into the black ceiling it floated under. The room pulsated with the sound of classical 21st century industrial music.

As Jarvis ran down the fire escape, some of the apartment's residents came out to gape at him. He ignored them. The drone scanned and eliminated face after face as it looked for Amanda Eden. Jarvis pulled out his gun and waited at the back door.

Eden sat at the corner of the bar and as the drone's camera zoomed in, she turned her head and looked straight at it.

"Shit," Jarvis cursed.

With a flick of her wrist, Eden sent a knife spinning through the air. Jarvis couldn't move the drone quick enough and the knife hit the wing. The drone spun out and the image of the club spun with it. Even over the music he could hear the screams of the crowd trying to avoid the damaged drone. Jarvis lifted his gun and pointed it at the back door. The door popped open and Jarvis heard a scream. A man twice Eden's size flew out at Jarvis; out of instinct Jarvis fired into the man's shoulders. Eden pushed her human shield into Jarvis like a battering ram.

Jarvis fell back into the alley and kicked the screaming man off him. He watched Eden jump off the lid of a dumpster and turn a corner into the crowed street. His drone came out the back door and despite its mangled wing floated over him.

"Go!" he shouted as the drone sped around the corner. Jarvis took off running, people scattering as they saw his uniform. Eden was a block away already, running people over and knocking them down. Jarvis's drone got into position over her as the Marine's drone flew up next to its left wing. Eden ran toward a food mall; a five-story building filled with restaurants.

Jarvis ordered his drone to dip over the crowd. Everyone dropped to the ground except Eden, who turned and extended a steel baton. She swung and bashed the drone into the ground.

"Stay down!" yelled Jarvis as he lifted his handgun. Eden smiled. She dropped the baton but slide a computer slide out from her shirt and into one hand.

"Hands up, Eden!" Jarvis pointed the pistol.

Eden put her hands up, still gripping the computer slide. Jarvis knew this was too easy. Something slammed into his back. He rolled on the sidewalk, past screaming people. He looked up to see a green drone flying just over Eden's as she ran into the street. She had hacked one.

The Marine's drone swept down and fired several rounds at Eden and her new, stolen drone. The green drone under Eden's control turned and headed straight for the Marine's drone. If they collided the tiny reactors would yield a devastating blast. Jarvis stood straight up.

"Eden, don't!" he screamed at her.

Her drone sped toward the Marine's. Hovering hundreds of feet above them, the team in the jumper braced for impact. It was too late, so Jarvis jumped and rolled under a parked taxi. The explosion was loud and it rattled the entire platform. With his hearing momentarily shattered. Jarvis rolled out from under the taxi. Flames and destruction spread out across the block. Over the haze of the heat, he saw Eden run into the food mall.

The entire front of the building next to it was burned away and the brick structure was falling to pieces.

Jarvis ran after her, jumping over the hood of a car in flames and a dead bicyclist. Inside the mall, Jarvis looked up. Five floors of various restaurants and seating areas spiraled upwards. Customers were screaming and scattering. Eden ran past the bathrooms under a sign that read 'Mall Offices.' Jarvis saw a second Marine drone in the street searching for them. He sent a location signal with his neural net and ran after her.

The hallway was narrow and several mall security guards ran out just as he entered. One did a double take and only saluted when he saw Jarvis's uniform. His hearing had returned but the hallway was silent. Jarvis had trained Eden, he had designed the combat programs she had trained on and thought he knew her plan. She would head out to the loading dock and try to disappear into the park.

Jarvis jumped out the door, and saw movement out of the corner of his eye. She was waiting with a pistol pointed at him. Jarvis lifted his gun and placed the barrel inches from her forehead. He could feel warm steel by his face. He looked into her eyes over the barrel of her pistol. Their eyes locked.

"Hi, Nick." Her calm voice pissed Jarvis off. He didn't reply and she held her pistol firmly. She watched for signs that he was going for his second pistol in the holster behind his back. He knew better; if they fired there was good chance nothing would be left of either of their heads. Jarvis didn't move, but scanned the alley around them as much he could. Wet ground, dumpsters, and less than a block from the entrance to the upper Golden Gate Park.

Eden shook her head. "I'm not going to prison."

"Well, you just made matters worse with that stunt out there, but there is a deal on the table."

"You think we can deal away our crimes? That's bullshit," she scoffed.

Jarvis wondered where the hell the Marine drone was. He

needed to keep her talking. Her pistol inched closer to his face. Jarvis tried to keep his voice steady.

"It's not much of deal. We do this job and you can forget about prison. Or don't do this job and they're talking about putting us on ICE."

ICE stood for Internalized Corrective Empathizer, but most people just referred to it as being out cold. The reality was much more sinister. In ICE, your body was not really frozen; it was a less-healthy, lower-tech version of hypersleep—it allowed your brain to dream while your body slowly decomposed. A program connected to your neural net induced the dreams, and these were not happy dreams. They were often a cycle of your crimes voiced over with surviving victim statements. No one has ever returned from ICE, and the rumor was that you could feel your body decay. Worse than the death penalty; it was legalized hell.

"Then I might as well shoot, right?" she said with a crazy smile.

Jarvis shook his head. Eden pulled the hammer back on her pistol.

"Since we're going to die, I just wanted say something..."

As she spoke a drone sped down the ally. Her eyes got wide and Jarvis jumped left as the drone fired. He rolled away as Eden's body collapsed. A bullet from her pistol fired past his head. Jarvis stood up and rolled her body over. Two darts stuck out of her back. Jarvis pulled them out and threw them on the ground before more toxins entered her body.

Jarvis looked up at the drone as it floated above his head. He stood up and slapped it. It spun around.

"Goddamn it I wanted to hear what she had to say!"

CHAPTER 5

JARVIS WAITED as the crowd of onlookers made room for the jumper to land in the street. A Marine blocked traffic on each side. Anderson took Eden's shoulders and Lambo lifted her legs and they walked her slowly to the open hatch. More people gathered as various clubs emptied to watch the drama.

As the sun rose, thunder from a storm to the west shook the platform. The wind picked up and Jarvis knew they had to get out before the sun fully rose. When the sunlight sizzled through the weakened Ozone, it warmed the ocean quickly. Daytime storms were so intense most of the west coast cities operated on vampire hours. The crowds would have no choice but to leave. The first drops of rain were already falling.

Jarvis kept his holster unhooked and scanned the crowd. He knew Garay was out there watching him. Suddenly, a red dot appeared on his chest. Jarvis followed the source of the light.

Jamal Garay stood at the edge of the crowd, his pistol under a coat to hide it. The laser sight was projecting from the tip of the bullet. Jarvis put his hands up and walked slowly towards him. Garay, a tall black man with naturally large arms and shoulders had spent hours sculpting them in the gym.

Nick Jarvis was big for a human but Garay towered over and intimidated everyone. It was the first time in years he had seen the large man and it triggered the nightmare he had been trying to suppress.

<<< >>>

They were on a mission on Titan. Eden yelled for him to get in there. Jarvis heard the screams; they sounded desperate. Jarvis ran down the hall and when he opened the door, Weddle glanced up and blushed like a child caught with his hand in a cookie jar.

The man from the union was tied to a chair. His blood-soaked clothes were wrapped in a ball by Weddle's feet. He had stopped screaming and his head dipped to one side. Jarvis didn't see Jamal at first. He was crouched down in front of the man, and there was pool of blood at his feet. The screaming man's lap was a bloody mess.

"Welcome to the party, Jarvis." Garayl's voice rumbled over the screams.

Jamal had something round and red that he rubbed on the man's lips like lipstick. Jarvis had walked through mass graves in his life but his stomach flipped when he looked closer. The man's penis and scrotum were torn open. Jamal turned towards Jarvis, smiling. As long as Jarvis lived, he would never forget that smile.

<<< >>>

Jarvis had trained Garay to be one thing—an agent of death. He had done too good a job, because there was very little left of the human being. Jarvis knew his only hope was to appeal to Garay's last shred of humanity.

He was almost to the curb.

"Stop!" Garay yelled.

Jarvis did as he was told. At this close distance, the bullet would rip through his armor like scissors through paper. The Marines suddenly came to life; rifles raised and laser lights trained on Garay. The maniac just smiled. Jarvis panicked; his emotional suppressors never worked around Garay. He got nervous like everybody else.

"Don't shoot, don't shoot." Jarvis locked eyes with him.

Garay ignored everyone else. The civilian onlookers wisely took off. The sky purpled with the first full rays of sunlight. The rain fell harder.

"Wake her up and let her go, Colonel," Garay ordered.

"I thought you were dead, Garay," Jarvis said.

It would have been easier if he had been. The war crimes tribunals had more warrants for him than anyone else. Garay was the one caught on camera using torture. He was the one with the biggest price on his head. He was also the one who had left a trail of dead bounty hunters.

"You broke her heart, you know," Garay spat toward him.

Jarvis did know. He had hurt everyone in his life. "It's over Garay. You can kill me, but there are enough guns trained on you to put down a squad. They have the whole team, we have to face the music." Jarvis hoped the man was listening.

Garay lifted his pistol until the red dot centered on Jarvis's forehead. Jarvis held his hands palm out to signal calm.

"The Colonel Jarvis who trained me was a go-down-fighting kind of motherfucker," Garay yelled.

Jarvis could barely see Garay in the glare of the red laser. He was close enough to knock the pistol from the man's hands. He considered it, but it was likely Garay would get a shot off.

Five years ago Jarvis would have been crazy enough to disarm him. But that was before he held Sammy in his arms. Before he watched his son grow day after day into a boy. Before he spent his son's second year answering every godforsaken 'why' question.

"I've changed, I have to get back to my son," Jarvis told him.

Garay grinned. "I thought I meant more than that to you. We all did."

Jarvis took a deep breath. "I know you can kill me and take out a few of those Marines but one or two of them are going to hit you." He pulled out a pair of handcuffs. Garay moved the laser and Jarvis was temporarily blinded. He expected Garay to pull the trigger and make his move.

Instead, Garay switched off the pointer. The red light flashed in his vision one last time as Garay spun the pistol around and handed it butt-first to Jarvis. He turned and put his hands behind his back.

The Marines handcuffed him and led him into the back of the jumper. Jarvis let himself breathe. Anderson walked up to him. "You were scared."

Damn right I was, Jarvis thought, but kept it to himself.

CHAPTER 6

THE GROUP of boys ran on to the remains of the playground. Every piece of play equipment was either covered in rust or broken in spots. It was so dangerous that if their parents were paying closer attention they would not be allowed to play there.

It was morning but the light was scarce. They called this time of day "shadow morning." These were the coolest hours of daylight and the only time they were allowed to play outside. The sun had climbed just high enough to be behind New York City. The massive metropolis was lifting inches at time but it had nearly reached the outer atmosphere. This provided northern New Jersey much needed shade. Even at night, it rarely dipped below 100 degrees on the surface.

The city had risen every moment of Sammy's five years. It was hard to believe that in a year or two it would be gone. Then they would get no relief from the power of the sun. After centuries together, New York City and New Jersey would be separated. He stared at the city in the sky and the halo of light behind it. It had been so much bigger when he was younger. He recalled sitting on his father's lap and watching the city. His father had promised his mother they would get citizenship to a jump-city.

"Come on Sammy," Matt called out as he ran to the wobbly swing-set. "My dad put up new ropes."

Sammy stopped at the edge of the playground and watched his friends fight over the two working swings. Dylan laid across the swing and pretended he was flying. Matt didn't mean to be a jerk but it made Sammy sad to hear him talk about his father. Sammy's mother had told him not to tell anyone that his father was gone, but the Jersey building was filled with nosey people. *Watch what you say Sammy. If people knew he was gone, it could mean trouble for us.*

He wanted to play, the laughter and smiles made him feel better, but his mother needed him. Their rations were getting low.

"I gotta go home." Sammy shrugged and walked away.

Kevin ran around him to block him. "We need at least ten to play football." He grasped an oblong ball held together with duct tape.

Sammy turned around and counted the boys left on the playground. There were nine. Kevin didn't like him and was never nice. Kevin's freckled face was constantly angry; a trait he shared with his father, Kevin Senior. Kevin needed enough guys to play five-on-five. He was older than the rest of them, and playing with him wasn't much fun. He changed the rules to make sure he won and when he had the ball, he ran over them like a truck.

The air was already getting hot, even in the shade of the city. Matt and Dylan were his age but smaller; Kevin was even harder on them. Matt stood behind the older boy, shaking his head. They wanted Sammy to take the blame for not playing.

Kevin lived in the same building as the rest of them. His parents had New York City standby citizenship, however. If enough people died in the city, they could get a spot. His father worked in sanitation, and had valuable skills. All the boys were instructed to be nice to Kevin but he was never nice to them. He had unkind nicknames for each of them: Dyl-head, Snatt, and Snotty for Sammy.

"I gotta go help my mom." Sammy tried his best to sound sad. It wasn't far from the truth; the water plant where she worked had closed down the previous week. The under-cities on the east coast were closing. The store where his mother traded for food and supplies was closing. A fight broke out over food last week and they were lucky to be eating lunch now.

He turned to leave. Kevin followed him. "Where's your Daddy, Snotty?"

Sammy kept walking.

"Anybody seen Snotty's dad?" Kevin taunted him.

Sammy turned and looked at all his friends. They were staring. Sammy felt the need to say something. His friends didn't believe him. His mind raced for a way to convince them. *He has been sick?* Then they would want to know with what? *He was on a trip? He joined the UN security forces and is fighting bad guys?*

None of it would work. Dad was just gone. He and his mother were alone, and the truth was they had no idea what had happened. He was angry with Kevin, but also with his father. What he said next just slipped out.

"Shut up," Sammy said just loud enough for everyone to hear.

Everyone was afraid of Kevin, so everyone was shocked. Kevin's eyes narrowed and Sammy took a step back. Kevin didn't respond. Sammy felt a little better. This time he raised his voice.

"Shut up!" His voice shook with emotion.

Kevin's lower lip trembled. He looked around and saw that all the boys on the playground had stopped and were watching them.

"I think your Daddy left you," Kevin whispered just loud enough for him to hear. "Maybe he got off-world, a one-way ticket."

It was the meanest thing anyone could say to kid being raised dirt-side. The gathered kids traded cringes and laughs. Sammy wanted to hurt Kevin. All the sadness he'd bottled in for the last few days boiled over. Sammy didn't even squeeze his hand into a fist before hitting Kevin. The bigger kid might have hit back, but Sammy jumped on him and rode him to the ground like a sled. He hit as many times as he could.

He heard Dylan cheering while Matt tried to stop Sammy. Sammy felt Matt's hands grabbing him, trying to pull him off. He heard parents screaming from the windows of their building. Kevin stopped resisting, but Sammy had no idea how long the fight lasted. He only stopped when and adult hand grabbed his arm and yanked him free.

Dylan's father, a wiry Asian man, nearly pulled Sammy's arm of its socket. Sammy looked across the field to the building he called home. Kevin's father was running toward them with a shotgun. Sammy turned to see several of the residents from the building raising their weapons as well. They formed a circle around Sammy and the other boys and pointed their guns at each other. People were starving and stressed beyond their limits.

Sammy looked down at Kevin's bleeding face. Matt's father cocked his shotgun.

Dylan's father raised his hands. "Calm down everyone, calm down."

Kevin Senior didn't lower his weapon. Sammy saw his own mother running from the building. She had his father's pistol. He tried to act tough but he silently prayed for his mother to get there quicker. He began to cry and through the fog of fear he saw something above them. A flash of light in the sky as a thread of sunlight poked through. A military drone on silent mode slowly approached them.

Kevin Senior kept his eyes on Sammy. "He just beat my boy."

"Kevin's a bully!" Dylan pleaded. Both fathers shushed him.

"Weapons down, now!" Melissa yelled as she got closer. No one responded to her. She cocked the pistol, putting a round in the firing chamber. Like most of the guns on Earth now, it was a century, if not several centuries old. The weapon's loud click got everyone's attention. Melissa waited as all eyes slowly turned toward her. "Anyone hurts my boy; my husband and I will kill everyone in this neighborhood."

"Relax Melissa, we can work this out." Matt's father lowered his gun.

"He ain't here, ain't nobody seen him neither." Kevin Senior kept his shotgun pointed at Sammy. Kevin Junior got up on his hands.

Sammy waited for his mom to respond but she took her time; seconds that seemed like an eternity. "I think you all know who he is. You've been real polite not saying anything."

There was a visible reaction to her words.

Sammy didn't know what she meant by *You all know who he is.*' He was only five but he learned to pay attention and put things together quickly. He tried think like a grown-up to help them survive. He wished he understood. He loved his father, he had cried himself to sleep every night since his disappearance. He wanted to understand what they were saying about him.

"He's coming back, and you all know just what he is capable of." Melissa's voice was quiet but hard. She looked around at each man.

Weapons came down slowly. Kevin Junior, now on his feet, moved toward Sammy but his father caught him by his shirt and pulled him back.

Sammy's mother was the last to lower her weapon. "You keep your son away from our boys. I don't give a shit if you might become a citizen. That doesn't help the rest of us."

Kevin Senior laughed and pointed at the city rising in the horizon. "We're getting out of here. You'll all be eating dirt, begging for our help."

He pushed his son back toward the building. In the distance, the market bell rang. Sammy glanced back up at the drone hovering above the scene. Dylan's father pulled out his computer slide. They were all getting weather alerts.

Dylan's father rolled the slide back into his pocket. "Come

on, we got to get inside. One hundred and twenty plus heat index," he told them.

The crowd wandered off. Bands of sunlight peeked around the skyline. Sammy waited for his mother as she slid the old pistol into its holster. He was used to seeing his father wear that holster. She grabbed his hand and they walked toward the building.

"I'm sorry, Mommy," he told her.

"That whole family is a pack of jerks. I understand. Just keep your distance."

Sammy pointed up at the sky. His mother stopped when she saw it. The drones patrolled the surface all the time, but it was odd for one to stay in one spot for so long.

"What is it doing?" he asked her.

"Come here you sons-of-bitches!" She screamed at the drone.

The drone sped effortlessly down to them. Reflexively Sammy pulled away but his mother held him in place. The drone floated at her eye level, close enough to kick up her jet-black hair with with its whirring wings.

"Why didn't you help him?" she asked the drone.

There was no response.

"You need us alive. I know you are using us to make him work for you," she spit out the words.

"Your son was never in danger," a disembodied voice projected from the drone.

"Where is he?" Melissa Jarvis lifted her pistol and pointed it at the drone. "Where is my husband?"

The drone lifted into the sky. Melissa grabbed Sammy's hand again and they walked in silence by to the building. He heard her choke back tears. He was angry; why wouldn't his father come home? They needed him.

CHAPTER 7

JARVIS SHOOK EDEN'S KNEE. The handcuffs snapped as Eden woke up and reached for him. The chains pulled tight, keeping her fingertips from touching his skin. The various law enforcement men laughed and she looked around the room. Eden tried to get up but fell back to the hard steel seat. Her legs were shackled as well.

"No use," Garay had his eyes closed. Despite the rocking of the aircraft, he was trying to sleep.

She looked at Garay and then back to Jarvis. "Where are we?"

"I know as much as you now." Jarvis knew they were at high altitude. He felt his ears pop.

"I don't see handcuffs on you," she whispered.

Sudden, rapid acceleration pushed them back against the wall. Jarvis looked over her shoulder out a window. A brown, dry horizon sat below them. It could be anywhere on Earth. A city in the distance zoomed closer but it was still miles off. Whether it was a permanent platform or a jump-city, Jarvis couldn't tell.

A door opened and Cooper walked in. Jarvis assumed it was a hologram at first, but then picked up the smell of the old man's sweat. He was wearing a UN flight suit. His wiry hair was long and tucked under a UN Command ball cap.

"Cooper." Garay opened his eyes and tested the strength of his cuffs out of reflex at seeing him.

"Welcome, Miss Eden." Cooper smiled "Mister Garay."

"Where are we?" she demanded.

"UN Earth Center, Dubai Platform," Cooper answered.

Jarvis took another look and saw the Sky Reach tower. The city's famous landmark was the tallest building ever constructed. If you had the time you could walk the stairs sixty miles into orbit. Space religions that considered the Sirius B colonization a mandate from God had a pilgrimage climbing step by step. The most faithful walked to the stars.

Jarvis stood up as they circled the tower. The jumper slowed as they neared a dock and linked hulls.

Cooper waited by the hatch until Private Anderson opened it.

The door slid open to reveal a long hallway filled with jail cells. Each cell had electric bars. A guard held a large M-25 pulse rifle and waved them in. Eden shook her head but walked into the room. Garay was next. Jarvis was allowed to keep his pistols; he knew he was supposed to deliver his prisoners. With one hand on Garay and one on Eden, Jarvis pushed them forward. Only one guard and Cooper followed them. The sound of their heavy footsteps in the prison thundered like drums.

Jarvis pushed Eden ahead and looked into the first cell. Cason and Weddle both jumped out of their bunks, shaking their heads. Cason came up to the bars but was careful not to touch them. Eden laughed at seeing Cason; Jarvis knew why. His nickname for Cason was "His Bad Penny;" he was a tough hombre who managed to stay alive despite being blown to hell more than once.

"About time, Jarvis," said Cason. "I had twenty credits on you coming back last night."

Jarvis watched Eden's face as she looked from member to member of their old squad, filling the cells. Jammer was an Italian-born, Mars raised tech expert and pilot who ignored them and tinkered with some electrical device. Strickland was the team's knife expert. Burnett, a thick-muscled, imposing black man didn't get up until he looked saw his cousin, Garay, who trailed behind Jarvis.

"Shit," Burnett whispered.

What little humor they felt about the reunion melted away. Not one member of the team didn't blame or fear Garay.

Garay stopped briefly in front of Weddle's cell. Weddle reached between the bars and put out his fist for a bump as Garay passed but they couldn't reach. As they approached the last cell on the left, two cell doors opened.

Zana stood in one of the cells. She smiled at Eden. The only other woman on their squad, she was a beautiful African with one-fourth Chinese heritage who had a British accent. Eden turned and looked at Jarvis. "The gang's all here."

Jarvis grinned.

The guard with the rifle waved the end of his weapon at Eden. She rolled her eyes and moved into the cell. After the door shut, the bars glowed. Zana hugged Eden. Jarvis watched them before turning around to the empty cell.

Cooper put his hands out for his pistols. "Don't worry, Colonel; you make the right choice and you'll get 'em back."

Jarvis handed the pistols over and turned to the cell. He realized that they expected him to go into the cell with Garay. Jarvis looked up at the man he had trained.

"I won't bite, I promise," Garay told him with a small smile. Garay went in and sat down. The handcuffs disappeared as Jarvis entered behind him. The electrified bars slammed to the floor. The guard pushed a button on the wall and Eden's chains disappeared.

Eden turned toward the bars; Jarvis sat down on the edge of a bunk. He felt her eyes on him and he looked back at her and his stomach churned. They had lived through worse spots for sure.

This was the first time they had all been together since that screwed up mission on Titan. Everything had gone wrong from the minute they took that off-world job. Other combat missions all over the solar system had gone fine, but not the Titan job. One of their most brutal missions since the Exodus, the insurgency in Argentina, had landed them with the nickname that would precede them from that time forward. After two years working whichever side of the conflict had the most money, Jarvis had gotten somewhat complacent with his team's work. Oversight was nearly non-existent and things got ugly. The nickname first appeared on a news site's opinion page. The headline read: *Butchers of Rio Gallegos are Nothing Short of Goddamn Killing Machines*. Jarvis read the headline, guilt eating away at him. Garay and Burnett thought it was funny. They both wrote *Goddamn Killing Machines* on their helmets.

The legends grew and the offers and the money increased. Jarvis accepted the name that brought with it the kind of respect they needed in their line of work. They didn't have a logo or a marketing budget. But their reputations were worth a lot of money. So when workers on Titan mining ore started organizing against Titan Corps, a trillion dollar multi-planetary corporation, a labor dispute became a big deal. Billions of dollars for roughing up a few organizers sounded like easy credits. *Who better to be professional bullies?*

The media on Earth hardly existed anymore except on the major platform cities. Since human life was shifting to off-world colonies, Jarvis and his killing machines had no idea the spotlight they would be under once they arrived on Titan in the Saturn region. If you lived in any of the Saturn nation-states, you could afford direct neural net access. Something that was a battlefield advantage on Earth was common life on the colonies.

Whenever cruelty was part of the gig, Jamal Garay was called to action. On Titan, he operated his own special brand of cruelty, and unfortunately for their team he did so for the cameras. He should have known the man he was interrogating was jacked-up with an implanted eye that shot perfect high-def video. The images were sent from Titan to Mars and in a matter of hours, the media had made a villain out of Jarvis and his team. Titan Corps and their billions of credits disappeared; UN arrest warrants were issued and even the Asian Block nations agreed to uphold them.

Wanted for the murder of four and the torture of a great many more, the *Goddamn Killing Machines* were finally in trouble and Jarvis knew it was best to break up the band. He gave them orders to hide, and for six years, they had gone dark.

Zana walked behind Eden and looked at Jarvis. He returned her gaze.

"I had credits on Garay killing you." Zana laughed.

"I don't give shit who bet on who," said Jarvis.

"I almost killed you in Santiago." Strickland called out from his cell.

"The whiskey and the heat index almost killed me in Santiago," Jarvis shot back.

Everyone laughed except Cason. "Bullshit. Laughing like old friends. Listen to you assholes." Cason threw his shirt against the cell bars. The electrical field popped and sizzled.

"I did this for our own good.. They have a deal for us. We won't have to hide anymore," Jarvis told them.

Cason looked at Weddle who mouthed the word 'bullshit.'

"Spare me your rubbish, Jarvis," Cason stepped as close to the bars as he could. "I don't want your deal."

Footsteps rang through the corridor. Jarvis walked up to the bars and glanced down the hall at Cooper. He had gotten rid of the pistol and returned wearing sunglasses.

Cooper stopped outside Cason's cell. "Mister Cason, if I were you, and I am pretty fucking happy I'm not, I would listen to Colonel Jarvis. Who, I might add, is just as much a prisoner as you."

Cooper walked down to the cell to face Jarvis. "I thought your team had more respect for you."

"They did before you sent me all over the solar system to arrest them." Jarvis shrugged.

"Oh, it's worse than that," said Zana. "Since you brought us here, they've been poking and prodding us like lab rats."

Cooper laughed. He shook a finger at Zana.

He turned so they could all hear him. "Listen up, all of you. I know you all think you're being thrown in the fire over Titan. Forget about Titan. You motherfuckers have left a trail of blood, guts, and death across a dozen moons and planets. Every single one of you has blood on their hands and don't bother denying it. I have files on each one of you scum fucks, and it ain't light reading."

Cason laughed. Cooper walked down to his cell and stared at him.

"Yeah, it's hilarious Cason. Though if I had two dozen governments wanting to execute me, I might not be feeling so fucking jolly." Cooper strode down the length of the cellblock while he yelled. "You people are knee-deep in shit so foul you can forget about prison. You have two options. Turn me down and I'll have you on ICE by the afternoon. How would you like reliving twenty years of victim statements? Believe me there are plenty to choose from; quite a rotation. Does that sound like a relaxing vacation?" Cooper stopped and looked at Zana and Eden. "You will be the next generation of Special Forces establishing order in the new colonies. I need every single one of you grunts or the mission is scrubbed."

Cooper let that sink in. He cleared his throat. "Now, direct your attention to your VR Environment."

In a jail like this neural net data-stream connections were suppressed, so Jarvis felt a jolt as the signal came through. Jarvis was suddenly standing in a different room, one that he knew was a virtual image, but that felt real. One at a time the members of the team appeared beside him. Cooper stood at the front beside a 3D image of a large planet. The image floated about a foot off the floor. It was a large, blue-green gas giant with a large set of rings wrapping around it's equator and two dozen moons.

"This planet is Beta Tanius. It's the fourth planet in orbit between the big star Sirius A, and a white dwarf called Sirius B. It's a gas giant; you can't tell from this picture but it's one of the biggest planets known to science. For centuries, astronomers believed Sirius A was a trinary star system." Cooper waved one arm as he explained the history of the planet.

Jammer stepped forward and nearly into the hologram. He stared at it with fascination. Jarvis laughed at the smile on Jammer's face. "This is where the jump-cities are going," Jammer said, turning to the rest of them.

Cooper nodded and stepped around the hologram to point at one of the large moons.

"Beta has over 90 moons with T-15, or Hermea, the second largest. Hermea is where the jump-cities are headed. It will be the home to the largest human colony off-Earth; at least that's the plan. In time the relocated cities will land in Hermea's massive ocean."

"You're going to have a population of at least a billion or two," Jarvis added.

Copper nodded. "It will be UN Controlled and not far away from the Asian Block colony on T-7. We suspect our war will not be so cold out by Beta. Two-way communication doesn't work, so oversight is also impossible. It could be the Wild West, it could be open war; this type of colonization is a gamble."

"Cooper, Beta is a nearly three hundred-year hypersleep trip." Jarvis stared at the image of the giant planet. "You're asking us for six hundred years, might as well put us on ICE. We have lives in *this* solar system."

Cooper stepped down and put his hand on Jarvis's virtual shoulder. "Well, standard technology has the drop ships and jump-cities maxing out at 3% percent the speed of light and yes, that would take two hundred and eighty-seven Earth years. That's relative time of course. But what if I told you I had a ship that could go 86% of the speed of light?"

Burnett whistled. Jarvis looked at Jammer, who shrugged his shoulders. "Nobody can go that fast," Jammer told him.

"We're talking a classified drop ship, not a colony seeder. One of the most advanced ships in our fleet," Cooper explained.

Jarvis turned back to Jammer. "You doing the math?"

Jammer nodded. "I suppose it's possible if his numbers are correct. It would take about ten years travel each way. Not sure exactly considering acceleration and deceleration."

Cooper smiled. Jarvis wanted to punch it off his face. "Two decades of your time, decades you will sleep through. Pretty good deal considering the war crimes your team has been collecting."

"Twenty years?" said Jarvis. "Some might say that's too good a deal."

"It's an excellent opportunity." Cooper pointed at the map. "I need your team at these new worlds."

Jarvis stepped closer to the image of Cooper. "Take our families," Jarvis demanded.

"I don't have to tell you the cost of citizenship in the new world. I can promise only you. You are welcome to stay there, or come back to see your son as an adult." Cooper turned away.

"His survival is not a guarantee," Jarvis whispered. He turned to Burnett who he knew had a family. "I'm coming home." Burnett nodded in agreement.

Cooper responded immediately. "Of course you can, but Earth is a shithole compared to the plans for Hermea."

Jarvis turned back to Cooper. "I'd like to talk over the offer with my team, in the flesh and in private."

Cooper snapped his fingers and the room melted away. Jarvis was back in his cell and the electric bars sizzled and disappeared. Eden looked more surprised than him at the open cells. Cooper was gone but his voice boomed from a loud speaker.

"You have five minutes to make up your minds."

CHAPTER 8

"Fall in."

Jarvis walked to a table that had appeared in the middle of
the hallway. Zana was the first to spin a chair and sit down.
Eden and Weddle came to the table; Eden was still rubbing the
raw skin on her wrists. Burnett and Cason approached the table
cautiously. Cason's earlier sense of humor had melted away.
Garay was in no rush; he was the last to come out the cell.

It was amazing how comfortable Jarvis felt around these
people. His father left in the Exodus for Tau Ceti when he was
ten and his mother was a huffer; she was always high. Jarvis was
only fifteen when he signed his UN military commitment. By
nineteen, he was leading combat missions. At twenty-four they
asked him to assemble his own team for off the book missions for
private contractors with foundation funding for enhancements
and training programs. They had the pick of the litter.

So began the year of recruiting and training. While Jarvis
never used the word family, it was always there under the
surface. He had hand selected them and knew their deepest
secrets. Weddle had been a ghetto rat in San Diego, a city that
never got a platform. It was an ugly place to live unless you
stayed on the coast. Weddle's very Christian pacifist parents had
been killed during a robbery at their small store that earned

their killers a grand total of forty credits. Jarvis had to wrestle with Weddle's shattered beliefs but he fit team's profile. Over the years Weddle had circled back to his parents' Christian upbringing and always had his eBible on him.

Eden had a mother, but they didn't get along. The older woman was a deadbeat who didn't want to earn her own money, so lived off her daughter's gymnastics talent. They traveled all over the solar system, the whole time at each other's throat. Jarvis had played Eden against her mother to sign her up.

Zana grew up in the Asian Block on the Johannesburg platform, one of six children. Her parents left during the second Exodus. Zana and her brother Jona were unable to get passes for the Exodus, so they both joined the UN military and were the only survivors of a battle six months into their UN service. Jarvis had recruited them both, and they remained together until Argentina, when Jona was killed during a fight. So Zana was alone now and like the rest of them, without family.

Until Melissa and Sammy, this group of warriors had been the only family Jarvis had known. He trusted them with his life more times than he could count. He had no idea the struggles that living on Earth would bring. He had not meant to have a child. It just happened. Everything changed for him, if he was being honest he didn't love Melissa like he had Eden, but he was trying to do that right thing with Sammy. He had done everything he could to get them off-world. He thought he had escaped the crimes of his past. Now they had to face them.

"Look, I'm sorry it went down the way it did, but if I asked nicely no one would have come in. I have reason to believe the Asian Block is still pretty hot about New Singapore. It was a fresh colony but the Asian Block's Martian command makes these guys here look like girl scouts."

Weddle looked down at the table. "I shot a kid in New Singapore."

"Shut your hole Weddle," Zana snapped.

Weddle lurched over the table at Zana but Jarvis locked eyes with him and pushed him back into his chair. Something wasn't right with the guy. Zana turned to Garay. "We all know whose fault it is that we're here right now."

Jarvis thought it was bold of her. Honestly, they were all afraid of Garay. The man didn't get mad or posture. He just smiled. An evil, sick smile. Jarvis didn't think Garay felt an ounce of shame. His actions had torn their lives apart and he didn't seem to care. Weddle looked at Burnett for a reaction. Burnett shook his head.

Weddle, Garay, and Burnett were close and always took point together. Weddle was alone in the room with Garay when things got ugly last time. Interrogation is always nasty, but Garay had a way of shedding his humanity that was hard to watch no matter how tough you thought you were. Jarvis had to keep a close eye on Weddle.

"We all have issues, and I deserve the brunt of the blame as your commander. But lock that shit down. We are short on choices, so let's figure this out. We should do the job." Jarvis looked around at each of them.

"So who are we even doing when we get there?" asked Strickland. He hung back at the edge of the group, next to Burnett. Cason was being too quiet; it made Jarvis suspicious.

"Let's not kid ourselves," said Jarvis. "They could've gotten anyone so I suspect that's a bullshit excuse. They've got something shady up their sleeve."

Jarvis looked at Burnett, the only other father. He knew Burnett's weak spot; vat-grown or natural, he considered children to be off-limits.

Jamal Garay and Donny Burnett were cousins who both grew up on the streets of Chicago under the shadow of the Windy City platform. Under-Chicago was an oven in the summer and it drove kids nuts. It wasn't easy to survive July in Chicago, so when Jarvis drafted Burnett, the young man suggested his tougher cousin. *He's a bruiser,* Burnett had said.

A week later Jarvis walked in front of an angry SWAT team there to bring them in. years later Jarvis wasn't sure how Burnett would react.

"I'm cool." Burnett whispered. "Just get me back to my girl."

"Ahh that is sweet. Mister Mom needs to get back to his girl," Garay laughed at his cousin. Burnett returned the dirty look, but said nothing.

"I know the length of the mission is not," Jarvis began when Cason suddenly yelled and knocked over the table. In a matter of seconds he had turned Jarvis around and held a makeshift knife to his neck. Cason nicked him under the chin so Jarvis understood how sharp it was and then pressed the blade to his artery. Everyone had jumped up and were standing tense; no one wanted Jarvis to die. Not now. Cason had rigged the blade from razors and pens and it was held together with plastic wrap from yesterday's lunch.

"Put it down, Cason!" Boomed a guard's voice as he ran in the room, rifle at the ready.

"Back off! I'll handle this!" Jarvis yelled and felt the warm edge of the blade close to his flesh.

The guard lowered his rifle and stepped backwards.

"What are you doing?" Jarvis asked in as calm a voice as he could.

"We all know they are lying," Cason bit out.

"Do we now?" Jarvis raised an eyebrow.

Cason turned his head to Eden, who was inching closer. She locked eyes with Cason.

"Put it down Cason," Jarvis said as he looked for a reflection to see Cason in. "Don't make me kill you, buddy."

"You want to go, fine. But not me—I am through taking bullets for someone else. There's no one to train; they send us in when they want somebody dead."

Eden stepped closer.

"Back off, Eden," said Jarvis.

"Yeah, back the fuck off," added Cason.

Eden put her hands up as if to say peace. On her arms were stainless steel wristbands and Jarvis saw Cason's reflection in them. Jarvis took a deep breath and nudged Cason back. The blade separated from his neck long enough for Jarvis to flip

Cason onto his back with a thud. Jarvis twisted the man's arm and grabbed the blade. He held it up to Cason's neck.

"What makes you think you have a choice?" Jarvis kept his eyes locked with Cason's. "It doesn't matter. None of it. We kill him, her, or whatever the motherfucker is. We kill it or we end up cubes."

Jarvis stood up straight and threw the razor into the closest cell. "There's not a lot to like about this plan. When have we ever gotten an easy gig? I don't like it but quit your whining and pack your shit."

Jarvis put out his hand for Cason. "We cool?"

Cason took his hand. "Nah, we ain't cool. Not until this mission is over and I don't see none of you ever again."

CHAPTER 9

MELISSA JARVIS FELT HER NEIGHBORS' eyes on her as she walked her son back into the building. The elevator had not worked in years; the power in the building was always flickering. She lead Sammy up the stairs to the third floor, his hand tight in hers. Dylan waited in the hallway for them and waved at Sammy before his father pulled him into their apartment. Melissa pushed Sammy inside but stared at the shut door for a moment. Life here was hell enough without drama.

Sammy ran to shut the blinds; the sunlight coming through the window would heat the room to unbearable levels. The building was constructed in the late 22nd century, during the last round of hope for environmental management on Earth. It was a hopeful time; Mars was being geo-engineered, so why not Earth? The apartment was built and wired to work automatically; she and Nick had to fix up the place to work analog. Even with central air the humidity was thick enough to slice.

Her only connection to the net was her computer slide; she pulled it from her pocket and unrolled it on the table. She looked for messages.

She had contacted every law enforcement agency they had spent years avoiding. She knew whom she married, but somehow she never thought he would get caught. She knew about the criminal accusations against him, but just wanted to know what they did with him. The drone watching them was the closest she had gotten to a response.

Sammy didn't go to his room. He stood, staring at her. It was heartbreaking. He never had a chance to be a child; at five years old he was a survivor and smarter than he had any right to be. He was also Daddy's boy. He didn't have many memories in his short life that didn't include Nick Jarvis.

"Where is he, Mommy?"

She had told him a hundred times she didn't know. She didn't want to say it again, so she just kept scrolling through the slide for messages. Weather alerts, pending ration applications, health warnings, and denied citizenship points filled the slide's screen.

"Why does everybody know who Daddy is?"

Melissa looked at her son. He stood still in the hallway, his eyes locked on hers.

"Why are they afraid of Daddy?"

She wanted to scream, to tell him to stop. She was sweating under the glare of her son, and the temperature didn't help. She walked over to him and kneeled down to eye-level. She rubbed the sweat off his forehead. It was moments like this when she got angry with herself. She loved him, but he deserved better than this.

"All that matters sweetheart is that he loves you."

He didn't smile. His face remained flat. "Then why isn't he here?"

Melissa didn't complete the sigh. Their front door exploded inward, a million flying shards of wood and plastic splattering over them. Melissa dove on top of her son and felt the shards pepper her back. The pain was instant but it was nothing compared to the fear. She reached for her holster and spun with the gun aimed up. She fired a single booming shot. The shot disappeared into the swirling smoke that had been their door. She kept the pistol raised as a drone floated through the smoke.

The second shot dinged the metal center of the drone. It

wobbled but stayed afloat as it sent an electrical shock through the air. Melissa felt the shock from her toes to the top of her head. She felt nausea overtake her before her legs gave out. Melissa dropped the pistol.

She turned around to see two UN Marines come into the apartment.

"Run!" Melissa screamed at her son, but he didn't move. The Marines pulled on their legs. Melissa looked up at the soldiers. She didn't have strength or control to kick them but she tried.

"We got 'em," one of them said.

Melissa fought to speak but couldn't muster words.

"Don't worry lady, they need you for something," The second one said as he hoisted her off the floor.

Then the world went black.

CHAPTER 10

Jarvis relaxed and looked out the window and waited for the artificial gravity to kicked in. Eden unhooked her straps and smiled at him as the lack of gravity lifted her. The Earth still took up their entire view but it would be gone in a matter of minutes. The longer he spent in space the greater he got a sense for the folly of generations past. The Earth is a rare jewel hanging in space. The stupidity of the 10,000 generations before them who never thought about how important Earth was. When you sat on a ship looking at it from space, a scarred, dead shell of what it once was, headed toward little bubbles of technology, the magic and wonder of Earth was overwhelming. It was a heartbreaking habit almost everyone had. To stare longingly as it grew smaller in the window.

It was a wonder the human race survived the dark days at the end of the twenty-first century. Wars fought over water helped combat the population crash, both sides putting the majority of funds into to warfare and survival schools, the advancement of science and technology actually went backwards for a time. The eventual peace was pragmatic, and in time the UN and Asian County Bloc let the war go cold to ensure the survival of the species. Scientists again directed their attention to space.

They were close enough that he could still make out the shape of Paris. The lights of the city flickered under the massive clear dome that encased the city. It was a breathtaking sight; the ancient city had become a starship.

They were lucky that Jupiter was on the same side of the sun in its 12-Earth year orbit. They would transfer at Io to a deep space hauler, and most ships took weeks to travel across the solar system. Unthinkable twenty years ago, but they would be there just a few minutes longer than an Earth day. The science was beyond his training and downloads. Not enough room in his implants or his natural brain for that nonsense.

Cooper walked down the aisle of the ship. He stopped at Jarvis's cell. "Better say goodbye while you can, Jarvis. Once we reach full speed we will be traveling at 3% the speed of light. You'll need to be in one of the pods during acceleration."

Eden turned away from the window and looked at Jarvis. "Goodbye to who?"

Jarvis didn't answer and stood up. The rest of the team seemed relaxed. Everybody except Weddle. Even Cason had begun get into the idea of the mission. Weddle had a reader pad with the eBible open, and was reading to himself. Jarvis watched him for a moment. Weddle stopped long enough to look up at him and then went back to reading.

Burnett came out of one of the holophone rooms; he was emotional from saying goodbye to his daughter. Jarvis grinned at him; Burnett grunted and joined his cousin by a window. Jarvis opened the door and stood in front of the camera. As he dialed the number, his neural net reminded him that it was 7:45 AM east coast time. After three rings, the room changed into a fancy apartment. Jarvis was shocked. He expected just an image of her face projected from her computer slide.

Sammy jumped up and down on a beautiful gray couch behind her. Melissa wore a strapless summer dress. She looked stunning but the most beautiful part was the smile on her face. The smile that the wastelands had beaten out of her years ago.

"Daddy!" Sammy was happy, but that wasn't odd. He was

wearing brand new clothes. That was impossible in the under-cities.

"Hey there, kiddo!"

Sammy ran up and hugged the hologram of his father. Jarvis squeezed the light and compressed air that represented his son. It was fake, cold, and hollow. It never fooled him, but he hoped it was enough for Sammy. Melissa sat emotionless on the couch. Something was off.

"Where are you Daddy?" Sammy sat down in front of the image of his father. "I'm right above you in orbit."

"In space! No way!"

"Yeah, I'm on my way to Jupiter for a job."

Melissa smiled. "That's amazing sweetheart, we are so proud of you; aren't we Sammy?"

Sammy nodded. "We are proud of you, Daddy."

Jarvis wanted to scream bullshit. Sammy had never been apart from him, and Melissa would never have been this happy to be left behind. Jarvis squinted at the projector.

"Is everything OK?" he asked.

"Of course," Melissa hesitated. "Look at this beautiful apart-ment the UN gave us. They just want you to focus on the mission."

"We'll be here when you get back, Daddy," Sammy assured him.

"I'm real sorry about it buddy, it may be a few years. I'm really going to miss you." Jarvis looked back down at his son.

"How long are you going to be gone, Daddy?"

Jarvis tried to speak but got choked up. "Ah...I don't know exactly, Sammy."

"Years?"

Jarvis nodded; he felt tears forming. "Yeah, I'm sorry bud. I want you to always remember that I love you."

Sammy was silent for an agonizing number of seconds.

"I swear Sammy, I am coming home, and we're going to do fun stuff. Just you and me," Jarvis told him.

Sammy nodded, but was crestfallen.

"Hey no matter how long I am gone, don't give up. I love you." Jarvis tried to smile.

"Love you too, Daddy."

Jarvis turned his eyes toward his wife. She had gone silent, and then as if given off-camera direction, she smiled as big as she could. "We are so proud. Focus on the mission sweetheart."

"One more mission Mel, and we'll be a family again." Jarvis forced himself to sound positive.

Melissa wiped away tears and sat silently until Jarvis was ready to scream. The room started to fade. They only had a few seconds.

"Is Eden there?" Melissa asked quickly.

Jarvis didn't say anything, he thought about saying no, but he had lied enough. He had no reason to lie anymore. The question made him angry. The holographic image snapped out for a second, the room was gone, then it returned, Jarvis wasn't sure if Melissa could even see or hear him.

"Just wait for me," he told her.

The apartment blinked out. Jarvis dropped his hands into his face. He took a deep breath.

"She's hot, Jarvis."

Jarvis turned to find Eden standing in the doorway. She had her leg propped up on a chair and a shit-eating grin on her face.

"What was it you said to me? Oh yeah, I remember. 'Civvies don't understand us, Eden.'" She mocked Jarvis's voice perfectly.

Jarvis knocked into her shoulder as he passed. Zana was behind Eden in the hallway and laughed as Jarvis walked past her. He went right to the bathroom, but knew he couldn't stay in the shitter until Jupiter. Jarvis took a long look at himself in the mirror. He didn't feel like a warrior anymore. He had a small scar beside his right ear from Argentina. He'd felt the bullet graze his skin but it hadn't slowed him as he rushed a machine gun pit. What happened to the man who bombed villages with drones, who shot one of his own men for disobeying an order? *Had a few years of home life weakened him?*

"What happened to you?" He said to his reflection. Jarvis washed his hands and sprayed water on his face. "Pull yourself together."

Jarvis thought back to the last six months. He never used to give shit about anyone... Saying goodbye was a part of the life he had chosen. That wasn't the problem. He knew when he said goodbye to the team on Titan, he was saying goodbye to Eden. When Sammy happened he had convinced himself it OK, Eden was gone. He loved Melissa, and in time he believed he would forget Eden. They would never see each other again. He assumed Eden had done as she said she would. Settled down.

Jarvis had replayed the conversation in his mind a thousand times.

"A farmstead on Mars, maybe off Lake Lomonosov. Land is cheap there." Eden smiled inappropriately for a woman who just found out they were wanted for war crimes.

"Lomonosov is pretty far north," Jarvis pointed out.

"Who is going to look there?" Eden shrugged one shoulder.

"So you're going to just settle down, grow potatoes or some shit like that?"

Eden laughed. Here came the part that haunted him.

"How about it?" She'd said.

At the time, Jarvis never considered that she was asking him. It was long after they had scattered across the various worlds of humanity that he thought back about it. He assumed she wanted to find some Martian farm stud. That her, "How about it?" was simply a question about the entire idea; not a proposition for him to join her. No, Eden had looked at him back then with the kind of love he no longer recognized. After years of war zones, death camps, and unending violence; longing, loving eyes spoke a silent language Jarvis didn't understand.

"Civvies don't understand us, Eden. It'll never work," he had

told her. He hadn't realized she wasn't talking about finding a civilian to live out her life with. She was asking him.

He never said goodbye; didn't even shake her hand.

Jarvis knew what bothered him; it was Eden. He had to put all that out of his mind if he was going to survive this mission. Jarvis opened the door and walked to his rack and picked the empty pistol case. It scanned his eyes and popped open. He looked over his shoulder. He lifted the velvet in the case and saw the hidden picture of Eden. She had been drinking that day at the beach. It didn't matter that she didn't understand. Now, for the first time in his life, he had a reason to survive; he had to get home to Melissa and Sammy.

He wanted to crumble the picture of Eden but couldn't. They would be at Jupiter soon. Jarvis unzipped one of the pockets on his uniform and stuffed the picture away. He would get back to his boy. That was all that mattered.

CHAPTER 11

JUPITER WAS a sight that never got old. Jarvis stopped to look at the massive planet from the open end of the hangar. After a moment, he picked up his pace to rejoin his group.

Their equipment rolled behind them on carts as they walked toward the deep-space ship. The spaceport on Io was built on an artificially flattened peak at the top of a mountain taller than Everest. The front of the bay was clear and nothing was between them and the view over the surface of Io. In the distance, several active volcanoes spit burning ribbons of lava. Past the moon's horizon, Jupiter spun like a colossal round pizza with giant strands of melted mozzarella pulling in every direction. The planet was a constant swirling storm of yellow and red.

The hanger bay was closed to all but UN personal; still the men and women working the spaceport stopped to get a look at the mercenaries trekking past them. The scorn and disgust directed at them wouldn't have bothered him in the past. That hatred meant big money in military contractor terms. Their reputation had earned them dirty jobs, and the credits for those jobs were always plentiful. The team was dressed in their standard gray and black uniform, which changed to camouflage if necessary. Jarvis fought the urge to smile back at the angry faces.

Burnett and Cason walked with their rifles at their sides; they were even less worried about their image.

Cooper waited for them by the hanger deck to the deep-space ship. He laughed. "You do realize you're just going into hypersleep for now, right?"

The carts rolled behind them filled with enough firepower to topple a small colony. Jarvis couldn't help it. He laughed too.

Cooper turned to the rest of them. "All right ladies and gentlemen, take a last look at your home system; it may be the last time. Stow your shit and get in your rack." The team scrambled up to the deck.

Cooper followed Jarvis into the ship.

"Did you get the all terrain vessel I asked for?" Jarvis asked the older man.

"Locked and loaded," Cooper said, still wearing his sunglasses.

They walked onto the deck of the ship; it was the size of a small cruise ship. Inside, Jarvis went up and rubbed the clean metal of the tank he had requested. He looked up; it was about the size of a three-story building. "I always wanted one of these."

Jammer looked up at it from a second-floor catwalk. "Holy shit, that's the AT-32 combat vehicle."

Jarvis snapped his fingers and pointed at Jammer. "Quit drooling and get to your rack, by the end of this mission you're going hate this fucking ship."

He laughed as Jammer caught up to Zana and Strickland, running toward the hypersleep chamber.

"I'm serious that fucking thing looks big now, but after a week..." Jarvis said as the team left the room. He turned to Cooper. He reached up and snapped the sunglasses off. "Take those stupid things off."

Cooper didn't flinch. They locked eyes.

"So we're locked in. No turning back now. Tell me, what's our mission? Our real mission?"

Cooper grabbed his glasses back and wiped them with his

sleeve. He turned to walk away. "That information is on a need-to-know basis. You don't need to know."

"The hell I don't. You expect us to do a job and I think that is exactly need-to-know," Jarvis yelled at his retreating back.

Cooper stopped and turned back to him. "Give me a break Colonel Jarvis. I am well versed in your data files; you have a long history of killing people who are nameless to you. This is just another mission for you."

"This is a lot of effort for a training mission."

Behind them, the giant cargo doors closed and sirens signaled that they needed to head up to the sleep deck.

"We are talking about the survival of the species, Colonel Jarvis. The control of not just a new world, but worlds...with an S. Worth more than the lives of a few war criminals and a couple billion in dollars. That is all you need to know." Cooper snapped his sunglasses back on.

"Launch in five minutes," the loud speaker squawked.

Cooper turned and resumed walking. "And in ten minutes we will be traveling fairly close to the speed of light, if we're not in the rack when we jump you will get sucked down a drain and reconstituted."

Eden and Weddle came up behind Jarvis as the ship rumbled to life around them. They stepped into the hypersleep chamber. Cason and Strickland were already naked except the tight underwear they allowed. The chambers were small metal pods that resembled coffins. Many in the service referred to them as coffins but Jarvis preferred to think of them as just good, old-fashioned racks.

"He's full of shit," Eden said and unzipped her uniform down the middle. Weddle did the same. Jarvis tried not to look directly at Eden as she stripped off her uniform...Jarvis stared at his zipper as he pulled it down.

"Yeah, I don't think they expect us to live," said Jarvis.

"We don't deserve to," Weddle said softly. Cason walked over and got in Weddle's face. It was easy to forget how huge the men on his team were, but with his shirt off, Jarvis could see Cason's ripped and imposing muscles. He towered over Weddle who was not a little guy either.

"We did our job. These UN hypocrites are just pissed because we did it for someone else too," Cason jabbed a finger at Weddle's chest. Weddle's arms stiffened and Jarvis stepped between them.

"Get in your fucking racks," he told them. Cason turned away and Weddle looked down at the floor.

Zana was the first in; the sound of her rack sealing and rolling back into the wall was enough to move Cason. He hopped up into his rack. One after another, the pods closed. Eden stepped up to the rack closest to Jarvis. They both sat with their legs over the edge of their pods, looking at each other. Cooper walked in already stripped down and loaded himself into a rack. Eden watched him too. The pod sealed.

"Something else is going on," Eden said. She pulled her legs over into her pod and grasped the top. "I've never been racked this long. Do you think we'll dream?"

Jarvis looked at her smooth skin and hazel eyes. He wouldn't be surprised to dream of her. He hoped to see his son and the home left.

Eden pulled the rack shut, not waiting for an answer. Jarvis looked around; he was the last one awake. He heard the ship's oxygen turn off. Around the ship all but vital systems clicked off. It was an eerie feeling as the ship went lifeless in space. It was the last step before all systems were re-routed towards the drive. Jarvis grabbed the lip of the rack and pulled it down.

The total darkness was extreme; there was nothing like this feeling. Even in the darkest of rooms, there was some light. The grunts always used to say, 'think about what you want to dream'. It never worked. His eyes felt heavy, his body relaxed. Jarvis took a deep breath and closed his eyes. He listened to his own breath and let sleep take over.

A scream, he heard a scream. Unformed moments passed over him like a wave, like a forgotten dream. He tried to remember. The pod opened. There were machines everywhere. Needles. Surgeries. Screams. Violence. Garay was angry. He battled robotic doctors. They never stopped.

Pods. More sleep. Oceans. As far at the eye could see. Virgin jungle. Soldiers. Children as young as Sammy. They called him SIR! Parts of his memories slipping through his fingers like sand.

Eden's hand on his shoulder. Her voice echoing, "It was all a lie..."

CHAPTER 12

HE HEARD a click and felt some kind of snap. Spasms wracked his body.

All a lie... the unspoken words echoed inside his head.

He opened his eyes to the pod's darkness. It was a natural reaction to fear waking in the middle of a journey. He prayed the pod would open; it unsealed with a hiss and he let out a relieved breath. If it opened during hypersleep every cell in your body would explode. A sliver of light poked in and stung his sensitive eyes; ten years in darkness was tough on the senses. Jarvis closed them and tried to control his breathing. He grunted and pushed as hard as he could.

A fully-dressed Cooper stood over the pod. Jarvis sat up sweating and looked around. The other pods were opening.

"What happened?"

"Welcome to Beta Tanius."

Everyone had the same natural reaction, fear of the pod opening during acceleration, and they fought to close his or her pods . Jarvis looked at his hands. He felt uncomfortable in his body. The dream he had felt like it only lasted a few seconds. Fragments of things he couldn't make sense of drifted around in his head.

"Holy shit," Jarvis whispered.

Cooper walked over and looked at the others in their pods. "Yeah, I told you technology improved, leaps and bounds, even in just the last few months."

Eden sat up quickly, Zana looked afraid. Cason tried to hide his fear.

"I thought we were cooked," Jammer said before laughing. It was a manic, nervous laughter. Cooper didn't seem to be showing any side-effects of hypersleep.

Jarvis was the first to jump down to the deck. The cold steel felt solid under his bare feet. He waited for his legs to give out or feel weak like they usually did after hypersleep. Instead, they felt strong. The others had gotten out of their pods as well, and were testing their own strength. Eden pulled on her uniform and Zana did a flip. Everyone laughed when she landed perfectly. She stretched her arms and her strong legs remained solid. Burnett flexed his muscles and nodded when he realized he hadn't lost any strength either. On a normal hypersleep trip, there were days of drugs, protein shakes, and rehab exercises before you were one-hundred percent.

Jammer walked through, passing out bottles with filled with protein drinks.

"I don't feel like we need these," Jarvis said as he opened it up and smelled it.

Cooper held his up and took a chug. He wiped some off his lip. "You need 'em. The pods are still experimental. It's not a traditional hypersleep. The computer has been stimulating and working out your muscles during the entire journey. I need you in peak physical condition."

Burnett glanced at the empty pod Garay had been in. He walked around the chamber and went into the bathroom.

A bar ran across the ceiling; a water tube or some kind of conduit, about ten feet off the floor. Strickland jumped and grabbed the bar with both hands. His biceps rippled as pulled himself up and down. He hit the floor and punched his open palm. "Ready to kick some ass."

Everyone but Burnett laughed. "Where the fuck is Garay?"

Jarvis looked at Garay's pod for the first time. He hadn't noticed it was already empty. The room grew quiet.

"Get into uniform." Cooper motioned them towards the door." Mission brief is in ten minutes."

Jarvis opened his drawer and saw his uniform neatly folded where he left it ten years ago. He pulled it out of the drawer. He felt odd. The hypersleep didn't even feel like a full night's sleep. He pulled on the uniform and zipped it up to mid-chest. He reached up to the pocket where he had left the photo of Eden. The pocket was empty.

He remembered it being there; he remembered putting it there. He considered checking the logs to see if anyone had been in his quarters but that was impossible. They had all been in hypersleep.

Jarvis shook it off and yanked the zipper closed. He was the first one into the hangar bay. The others joined him one at a time. The room was dark beyond the one spotlight shining on the AT-32. The ship turned. The outside wall of the bay had a window the size of a building and as the ship turned the view of the planet came into focus and lit the room.

The planet took up almost the whole window. It was crowded between moons, giant star ships, and rocks floating in its rings. It was not going to be easy flying. The planet was so massive the glow off it was as bright as direct sunlight; Jarvis held his hand up and peeked around it. Ships flew everywhere; the activity was amazing. It reminded him of the colonies around Jupiter.

Jarvis snapped his fingers at Jammer. "We need a pilot on the flight deck to get us into orbit."

Jammer saluted and took off for the command center.

Jarvis grinned at him; the Goddamn Killing Machines didn't have a chain of command. Jarvis had always been in charge but he never asked to be called sir. Still, old habits die hard and some of the team used that term on occasion.

Cooper sat at a computer close to the thin transparent field that separated them from space at the end of the bay. He tapped at the keyboard and directed five other programs with his neural net.

"Where is Garay?" Jarvis asked.

Cooper didn't look up just kept working.

"Answer me, Cooper!" yelled Jarvis..

Cooper spun around and pointed behind Jarvis. "You really don't want to miss this."

As the ship turned, they saw the closest moon—Hermea. Jaws dropped at the sight. The traffic in orbit was intense, including several ships and large orbiting space stations. The moon looked more impressive than Earth had since the first exodus in the twenty-second century. This much activity should not happen for a few more centuries. The UN must have had more high-speed ships than he realized.

Jarvis locked eyes on something familiar; a city in orbit. It looked like one of the jump-cities but its base was scored with dust and damage. It looked like the worn version of Paris he had just seen in Earth's orbit, but that was impossible. They hadn't been in hypersleep long enough for the Paris to have made it out this far.

"I'm updating our computers and neural net access to modern and local channels," Cooper said as his fingers danced over the keyboards. Jarvis watched as Hermea came within several million miles. They passed over the night terminator. There were lights everywhere, like stars. The population had to be enormous. Jarvis could feel something wasn't right.

"Colonel Jarvis, perhaps this is good time to..." Cooper smiled nervously. The loud speaker crackled to life.

"Hey Jarvis, I need to speak to you on the flight deck," Jammer shouted.

Burnett and Cason looked at Jarvis who turned to Cooper.

Jarvis stepped forward, anger flashing in his eyes. He was beginning to put things together.

"Don't bother," Cooper took a step back. "I'll tell you."

Jarvis stepped carefully into Cooper's face. "Tell me? Tell me what?"

"I can assure all of you, it wasn't my idea and I strongly argued against it."

Burnett stepped closer towering over Cooper. "Argued against what?".

The confidence with which the UN man carried himself didn't melt away as three of the toughest military contractors in the universe stepped closer to him.

"Before I tell you, let me remind you that I have neural access to the ships command codes and if my heart stops or my brain is too damaged to signal the ship, then...well the ship will self-destruct."

Eden laughed. "Oh boy, this is going to be some seriously fucked up news."

Burnett reached over Jarvis and picked Cooper up by his uniform. Jarvis tried to hold him back, but Burnett slammed Cooper against the force field at the edge of the bay. The glass responded to the pressure rippling like water rolling away from a dropped stone. Jarvis thought they might fall into open space for a moment, but the bubble didn't burst. Cooper grunted in pain, Jammer called Jarvis again over the loud speaker. Jarvis took a step towards the flight deck.

"Don't kill him... yet," Jarvis said, pointing at Cooper.

Burnett nodded. Cooper shook his head.

"Wait, I said I would tell you, just put me down."

"Fuck that, talk," said Jarvis.

Burnett didn't lower Cooper.

"It wasn't my idea, I told them to tell you. Technically speaking, I didn't lie about the amount of time. The mission is only going to take a short amount of your waking relative time. By law, any time spent in hypersleep is void in contracts."

"Son of a bitch," Cason said and ran towards Cooper. Zana stepped in his way. Burnett's eyes got wide.

"Where the fuck is Garay?" Burnett said. He was angry but didn't break a sweat containing it. "How long motherfucker?"

An image of Sammy played in Jarvis's mind. He jumped forward and pushed Burnett out of the way grabbing Cooper and throwing him to the floor. The wind was knocked out of him and he gasped.

"How long, you son of a bitch?" Jarvis growled.

"Your body only aged two years and thirty-three days. Look, I didn't lie! If you fucking grunts knew anything about space travel you understand going 86% of the speed of light is impossible." Copper laughed, a strangled, nervous laugh. "Really people don't even keep track of Earth years here, it's irrelevant."

Burnett kicked the window by Cooper's head. Cooper flinched as the window rippled again. Jarvis continued to hold him down. He dug his knee into Cooper' stomach.

"Irrelevant? I promised my son I would be back you fucking bastard."

"I told you not to make promises. You were never going to see him again. I knew that would be hard for you to accept."

Jarvis heard the curses going around the room. Cooper stared into his eyes. Jarvis knew Cooper was one thought away from ending the whole thing.

"Break his fucking neck, Jarvis." Jarvis was so focused he didn't even know who said it. He didn't think he could do it fast enough, or he would.

"I'll blow this whole thing to hell," Cooper whispered. Jarvis let go and stood up. He could've fought but every plan ended with them being blown to atoms. He swung his arms, indicating for the others to stay back.

"Don't worry about your kids, your parents, your fuck-buddies. Forget them all." Cooper stood up and wiped himself off. "They are fucking dust now, billions of miles away."

Cason pushed forward this time and Weddle and Eden had to help Zana hold him back.

"Don't blame me either, if you weren't here you would've rotted away as cubes. So don't cry to me about what you lost. Ancient history, those people had lives that ended three hundred years ago on a dying planet."

"It's the twenty-sixth century?" Cason whispered.

"Approximately. I'd have to verify using star charts, but they use a different calendar here in the Sirian system. Century three I think." Cooper paused. "It's better for all in involved if we just move on."

Jarvis nodded and muttered something. Cooper looked around the group and rubbed his hands together. "Think about it, back in your time you were hated, wanted criminals. It's for the best, really, if we move on."

Jarvis nodded again.

"OK, then." Cooper nodded, smiled and sighed in relief. "Are we cool?"

Jarvis punched him. Cooper hit the window hard and the screen rippled for the third time. Jarvis grabbed his shirt and the now-broken glass in the right side of his sunglasses trickled to the floor. A little tear of blood rolled down from the UN man's eye. He looked right at Jarvis but spoke to the whole room.

"I deserve that, but it's the last one. I want you fucking savages to listen, and listen good."

"More lies?" said Eden. "Where is Garay?"

Cooper's heart nearly beat out of his chest. Jarvis could feel it under his clenched fist. "I am more than ready for you fucking pukes to test me."

Jarvis felt a sharp pain in his head. He fell to the ground and pressed his hands to his temples. In a matter of seconds, it was over. He looked up at Cooper.

"How about Zana?" Cooper spit out. As he said her name, she fell to the floor and held her head as Jarvis had done. Just as quickly, it was over.

"Enough play time," Cooper threw his busted glasses on the deck. "I am linked to every skull in this unit, so the next time any of you barbarians touch me, I'll turn you inside out. Colonel

Jarvis, do me a favor and call this chickenshit outfit of yours to attention."

Jarvis stood up and looked at his team. Jarvis pulled his uniform straight. "Attention!"

The Goddamn Killing Machines straightened as one unit. Cason sighed deeply and looked away from Cooper. He couldn't look at the man. Jarvis felt the same, but lifted his head to stare at Cooper.

Cooper locked eyes with Jarvis. "The training mission is over. We have a fugitive who needs to be captured or killed. Complete this mission and your contract is settled. This is a military mission and I defer command to Colonel Jarvis on such matters. But do not fucking forget who the fucking man is." Cooper sounded tough but Jarvis heard fear in his bark.

CHAPTER 13

THEY HAD JUST under twenty-four Earth-hours before they entered orbit around T-13. Most of the team worked out while Burnett and Cason went to the firing range. Zana and Strickland sparred in the mat room. Eden ran the corridors. Jammer checked out all the drones and then the controls on the AT-32.

Cooper had avoided Jarvis. Refused to answer any questions. They all needed to calm down.

Jarvis sat in the galley reading the updated maps of their new solar system. His pistol sat on the table in front of him.

"How you holding up?"

Jarvis jumped in his seat and put his hand on the pistol. When he saw it was Eden standing in the doorway, he slammed the pistol into his holster. He avoided looking at her.

"Why did you have your gun on the table?"

Eden walked into the room and sat down. She offered her hand. He didn't take it. She sighed and said, "You can't blame yourself, you believed you could get back to him? Right?"

Jarvis was confused. He needed control of his team and he knew they couldn't trust him in battle if.... It hit Jarvis that she wasn't talking about Jamal Garay.

"What was his name? You said son, right?" She asked him.

Past tense. It was a mind-fuck. A week ago, Sammy had

been a little boy sitting on his lap. If he was lucky, Sam Jarvis died at least one hundred and fifty years ago. Sammy grew up without his dad, probably got married, had kids of his own, his children had children. In all those long years his only bitter memory of his father was a broken promise to return.

"I left them in hell," Jarvis spit out.

She stared at him.

Jarvis shook his head. "Aren't you supposed to make me feel better?"

"We all feel like shit right now." She shrugged.

Jarvis heard the voice of his first trainer at the academy, Sargent Morrell, in the back of his mind. His famous advice about emotions, 'You better use it, but if not bury that shit deep.'

Jarvis looked as seriously as he could at Eden. "It's buried now."

"OK, point taken," Eden grinned. "While we are having this heart to heart there is something else we need to talk about. In private."

"Private?" Jarvis was skeptical.

The door opened and Zana led the team in. One by one, they went up to the computer to order food. Jarvis looked at his watch, still set to Earth time. It read 9:30 PM. It was time for his mission brief. The table filled up around Jarvis as everyone sat down. Cason opened biscuits, while Strickland stirred gravy into mashed potatoes. Weddle strolled in last. Jarvis wasn't sure Weddle had eaten since they woke up. He would have to talk to him about that.

Jarvis stood as Cooper walked into the galley. The conversation halted.

Cooper put his hands on his hips. "So, what do you want to hear—the bad news, or the worse news?"

Strickland raised his hand. "Can you direct me to the beaches on T-13?"

No one laughed.

Jarvis put his hands behind his back. "If you're going to waste my time kiddies, only funny jokes allowed. One more of those Strickland and you'll be doing push-ups till we drop planet-side."

Strickland put up his hands to signal point taken.

Cooper opened a 3D holographic map that floated in the room.

"T-13 is a moon of Beta. Well, it's a planet, really; bigger than Earth but it orbits Beta like any other satellite. It's one of five moons with oceans, plant life, and oxygen."

"How is that possible?" Jammer shook his head.

"Not my field," Cooper shook his head. "They exist in the habitable zone entirely because of Beta's radiation. Don't worry, your food has been dosed with rad pills from the moment we entered the planet's magnetic field. Hermea will take a few decades of biotech engineering to make it perfect for human life but T-13 is as close to Earth as we have seen, no engineering needed."

Jarvis stared at the planet as it circled in front of him. The oceans were huge and there were only three continents; one that looked as big as all three Americas.

"If thirteen is so perfect why build the colony on Hermea?" asked Jarvis.

"Ever have one of those days where it feels like the whole universe is out to get you?" Cooper stopped the rotation of the T-13 image. He pointed at the large landmass on the planet. "Tartarus has a perfect atmosphere, but it also has an ecosystem that is hostile to human life. It's just a very dangerous place."

"So answer me this genius. Why the fuck would we want to go there?" Cason didn't smile. "ICE sounds better all the damn time."

Cooper stepped around the table to Cason. Jarvis didn't expect his soldier to be this bold. "Mister Cason, I'm giving you a chance to live free. You just have to find my fugitive. He has similar training and skills and is wanted for very serious crimes. We believe this target has chosen T-13 to hide and we had assumed the planet would take care of the matter but it seems against all odds the target is still alive."

"Where is my cousin?" Burnett said as he stared at the holographic moon.

Weddle lifted his head suddenly. "It's him, isn't it?"

Eden leaned back in her chair. "What the fuck happened while we were out?"

Jarvis held up the pad he had been studying. "The ark ships and the first jump-city are here. The colony on Hermea has the largest human population known to the UN. At least bigger than anything we had back in the twenty-third century." Jarvis let that sink in, no one wanted to show frustration at first. Eden blew out a sigh and shook her head. Jarvis nodded and looked at Cooper.

Cooper used his hands to zoom the floating map out. "The UN won the race but not by much. They didn't know what we would find here, so functioning colonies are actually good news. The Asian Bloc has a colony on T-5 called Wu. It's big, but information is sketchy. Outside of those bastions of civilization, the moons of Beta are pretty much a lawless chaos. There are various projects of biotech engineering in progress. Being cut off from Earth hasn't changed the general mood, the UN and Asian Block cold war is actually red hot out here. That shouldn't affect us on this mission."

No one was happy about this report. Cason and Burnett had the most trouble hiding their anger. Jarvis gave them a stern look.

"What is the real reason everyone is afraid of T-13?" asked Zana.

Jarvis grinned and shook his head. "Yeah that is the strange part, T-13 has an Earth-like atmosphere: humid, but oxygen rich."

Cooper added. "Survival is a challenge, the target is the first human to survive that we know of."

"So it is Jamal," Burnett said in a deep voice.

Cooper didn't respond.

"What about drones?" asked Jammer.

"They don't last long either, and before you ask there isn't much in the way of satellite footage. The moon's orbit of Beta takes about six Earth days. Given how close to the planet T-13 is you can go several Earth days on the light side. Sirius B has a six-Earth-year orbit but don't worry about it now as it is on the far side of A at the moment. That means nightfall is total darkness. Pitch black. The gravity of Beta is intense; it's why the oceans on T-13 are constantly nuts, the gravity creates crazy storms. Plus the rings are made of moons that already fell into the planet."

"Into the planet? Like boom?" Cason laughed sardonically.

"Yeah, like big boom, and that means moon rain, which explains why satellites have a rough go of T-13 orbit. So I know it's not much, but these are the pictures I have." Cooper uploaded satellite footage of the jungle and passed it on to their internal servers and everyone watched the video in their personal nets. A large river cut through a jungle. Large birds crossed the footage but mostly it just looked like a river.

"Asian Bloc discovered this river. They call it Nandu. The UN calls it the Red River, and the intel says our target has been moving along this river, somewhere hidden under the canopy."

Strickland laughed. "That's it. We take an alien cruise down this river, pop off a mark and we're free."

Zana smiled at Strickland. He didn't get it.

"That sounds like fuckin' cake to me." Strickland rolled his eyes.

Burnett shook his head. "Garay ain't no a cakewalk."

"No one said it was Garay," said Eden.

"No one said it wasn't neither," Weddle sounded scared. "He ain't here." He waved his arm around the table.

"Shut the fuck up," Jarvis slammed his fist on the table. "It's crystal clear I am the only motherfucker in this squad to download the file on that little cruise. That river is about twelve times longer than anything like it on Earth. The roof on that forest is thick, and filled with aggressive carnivores, who apparently think we're delicious."

Everyone was silent.

"This is one fucked up world." Jarvis tapped the table. "There isn't much, but read the fucking file. The drop alone is batshit, and has a death rate pretty damn close to perfect."

Jarvis looked at Cooper and jerked his head for the older man to follow him. "Now!" Jarvis stepped into the hall and the door closed behind Cooper, leaving them alone.

"You want to know who the target is?" Cooper asked him.

"If it is Garay tell me now because putting a tag on his toe will not be easy."

"I have faith in you Colonel Jarvis," Cooper walked away and didn't look back. "I have faith."

CHAPTER 14

JARVIS MADE sure the rest of the team were locked in before he walked up on to the small bridge. Cooper and Jammer strapped themselves into the pilot seats. Eden was strapped in as well. She ignored him, keeping her eyes on the front windshield. Eden knew she was the smartest person on the team after Jammer, and always tried to get to the front of the line, to stick her nose into decisions. As unofficial commander it should have bothered Jarvis but Eden enjoyed that privilege because he had trouble telling her no.

The hanger bay was already open, and the space outside looked well populated with ring debris. There was an intense roar as the oxygen in the hanger bay was sucked out, then nothing except the intense silence of space. Jarvis sat down and locked himself in just as gravity from their base disappeared.

Cooper turned to look at him, his stringy hair floating in the zero G. "Descent on your command, Colonel?"

"Jammer, what is our favorite saying at a time like this?" Jarvis asked his pilot.

Jammer engaged thrusters and the drop-ship pushed away from the base ship. They moved into the eerie silence.

Jammer smiled. "Getting old is for assholes, sir!"

Jarvis pounded his right fist into his chest.

"Indeed." More than ever, Jarvis added to himself.

It was a silly tradition, but important to Jarvis. For years, they have gone into situations like this, for something as meaningless as UN credits. They had lost five members of the team and a few limbs but at some point you had to tell yourself life was not that valuable a gift if you were going to function in this career. It was easier the further and more disconnected humans were from Earth.

Quaint old ideas of religion have not died out but they have faded. The Earth and human birthright in the universe felt more and more like an accident. It didn't matter if you were piloting a drone or pulling the trigger on an AR-60, it didn't help if you believed in the value of life.

Value credits, not life, and at the end of the day you'll have an ass to relax on.

Jarvis had relaxed enough to close his eyes when the ship swerved violently.

They had passed a small section r of the rings. Jammer swerved the drop-ship to avoid a rock the size of the ship. He whistled and turned on music. It was too quiet for everyone. Jammer moved the ship to the electronic beat playing off his personal net. The ship avoided rock after rock until they got a direct shot to T-13. Everyone relaxed.

Their deep-space base ship would have to hold in an orbit higher than the rings. Still, it was likely to take a beating by random pieces of moon rock. After the drop ship deposited the AT-32, the on-board AI remote pilot would return it to the base ship. It wouldn't survive in orbit on its own, and having the extraction ship so far away made Jarvis nervous.

Jammer increased the speed in the direction of T-13. As it grew closer, Jarvis noticed it resembled Earth. A large blue ocean with swirling storm clouds and a continent that stretched from the tip of the southern hemisphere to the north. It was like looking at a face you knew but with one feature slightly different. They spent most of the two-hour trip in silence as the moon loomed larger and larger in their view. They were entering the upper atmosphere, when you could make out the long river cutting from the northern tip of the land mass for tens of thousands of kilometers far into the south, where it dipped back into the ocean. They silently watched it loom larger as it took them ten minutes to drop through the first fifty miles of the atmosphere.

"My god, it's huge," said Eden.

"It's one thing to read about it." Cooper smiled.

The ship shook as they cut into the atmosphere. The windshield glowed red as they burned through. Jammer looked at Jarvis who hit the intercom.

"Prepare for final entry." Jarvis sent the warning out.

The light changed and it looked like dusk as they rocketed down. After a few minutes, the sky brightened around them. It wasn't quite as bright as Earth but the ozone was in better shape. The light bounced off the planet towards the moon's surface. Far below, it looked solid green.

"Sixty-five thousand feet and dropping," Cooper said as he watched the sensors.

It didn't feel like they were moving fast at first, but the green of the T-13 surface grew in their sight. Jarvis wasn't a great pilot, and he hated the feeling of not being in control.

"Sixty thousand feet," Cooper announced.

The ship shook slightly but was dropping smoothly. Jarvis tried to enjoy the feeling.

"Once we get in the AT, things will get bumpy. Fifty-five thousand feet." Cooper kept his eyes on the controls.

The gravity increased as Jarvis felt something pressing him back into the chair. He unhooked his straps. Eden did too; Cooper looked around and nodded.

"Fifty-thousand feet!"

Cooper and Jammer unstrapped, but Jarvis and Eden were already at the door. They ran down the hall and Jarvis opened a hatch in the floor. Jarvis went first, dropping into a narrow tube slide. He came out in a room where the rest of the team was strapped in. Eden, Cooper, and Jammer all slid into the room. Jarvis sealed the hatch, as the others worked to get strapped in.

"Detach!" Jammer warned them.

There was a loud cranking, followed by a snap. The drop-ship spit out the AT-32 like bad medicine. The giant tank dropped faster than the drop-ship. It spun a little in the air. Jarvis looked out the window and saw a split-second view of the drop-ship bursting like a dart back to space.

"We're free from the drop-ship, forty thousand feet," Cooper told them.

Jarvis felt pulled across the room. He reached out to grab a strap. They hit a massive air flow jet stream. Suddenly the whole thing spun like a dreidel. It felt like being inside a clothes dryer. They needed to get to at least 30,000 feet before they could deploy the parachute. Jarvis struggled to get into the straps.

"There had to be an easier way," Cason screamed. Jarvis knew he hadn't read the file. High in the atmosphere, there were large predator birds the size of starships. They are blind but it is believed that they sensed the movement of other flying creatures that they deemed big enough to eat. They didn't react to something simply dropping, but if it moved aerodynamically, the first reason this moon is not desirable for a colony becomes obvious.

Jarvis snapped the straps in.

"Thirty-thousand feet! Hold on!" Cooper screamed as Jammer unleashed the parachute. Everyone grunted as the chute opened and the ship's spin slowed down. Their descent slowed. Still the wind roared louder than anything Jarvis had ever heard. Zana rubbed her head.

"This is giving me a headache," she said to no one in particular.

Jammer clapped his hands once. "One of those fucking birds came after it, but the drop-ship made it back to orbit. En route to base ship."

Cooper activated one of the hull cameras. He watched the video inside his neural net and shared with the whole team.

"Oh shit." Cooper gritted his teeth.

A giant winged dragon-bird sped through the air towards them. It was about 10,000 feet below and a few miles to the north. It looked to be the size and length of a Martian Bullet Train; it's teeth were sharp and the size of cars. Even in the distance you could see blood stains on its mouth and teeth. It moved like a bird but was more like a dinosaur.

"It's a goddamn dragon," Jarvis whispered.

It didn't have eyes but it sensed their movement and flew towards them. Weddle cut off his server and closed his eyes out of raw fear. Jarvis could see his lips moving, some kind of prayer.

The chute pulled better with each second, which was a problem; they were slowing down into the path of the dragon-bird. They were just ahead of it, close enough for Jarvis to snap stills with the outside camera, it was green and had the wing-span the length of a football field.

Another Dragon-bird dipped down to catch them.

"Cooper," Jarvis yelled. "You said it would think we were something dead, it would ignore us."

Jarvis reached over Jammer to the controls.

"No!" Cooper reached over blocked his hands. "We thrust and it will only come harder! They only eat living prey on the move! We have to look dead."

Cooper directed the camera at the back of the tank. The parachute took up some of the view but the sky was filled with those dragon-birds. They swirled overhead like vultures over a massacre.

"Holy shit, those are fucking dragons," Cason said over nervous laughter.

"Nothing we can do," Cooper grinned. "It's just a bird."

Jarvis leaned back and expected to die. So far from home, disconnected from his family forever. He felt a burst of rage at the waste of it all.

A boom shook the tank. The tank slowed in its descent as

the powerful chute collected air. The cameras spun and every one streamed different images. The dragon-birds had flown over. Jarvis looked out the window. The view was shaky as they continued to fall. Whatever made those things think they were alive must have ended when their descent slowed. Jarvis saw them shrinking into slow dots against the horizon.

"What happened?"Eden asked.

"They're gone," Jarvis told them.

CHAPTER 15

JARVIS ENJOYED THE SLOWER DESCENT. He engaged the cameras to get a better look. The jungle canopy was thick. Giant trees reached 1,000 feet in the air and made seeing the surface almost impossible. Jammer did his job perfectly and they were heading toward the ocean a kilometer off shore. The lip of the river was not clearly defined. There was a swampy delta of massive trees rising out of the ocean. The trees swayed under a strong wind.

Jarvis stared at the delta as the tank lowered itself towards the water.

"Everyone brace for impact, I'm releasing the chute," said Jammer.

Jammer clicked off the camera view, and released the chute. There was whopping sound and they dropped fast. The crash into the ocean shook them violently but in seconds, it was like being back in the silence of space.

"Jammer, switch to submersible mode," ordered Jarvis.

The tank groaned around them. The AT-32 was developed to be the ultimate combat vehicle, able to function in any environment, from deep space to the darkest depths of the ocean. It could shift from space vessel to submarine to land vehicle in a matter of seconds. The only drawback was that if you were anywhere but the control room, you could easily get sliced to pieces. That's why they designed the tubes, so you could drop in if you needed to.

Jarvis turned the external cameras back on. The ocean swam around them, teeming with unusual life. Gasps erupted around the control room as members of the team found the camera feed. Three large creatures swam up to the camera. They went right to it. It was like they were looking back at them. They looked like an octopus, small body with eight tentacles. Jarvis signaled the camera to take a still.

DON'T!

Everyone grabbed their heads, after feeling a sharp pain. They didn't hear the word; they felt it, like a jolt of pain. Jarvis looked up at the monitor. The octopi-creatures were gone. Jarvis and Eden shared a look.

"What the fuck was that?" Asked Eden.

Eden shook her head in disbelief.

"The question becomes, does that thing breath air, or do they remain in the water?" Cooper unstrapped himself.

"Look alive, we're almost to the surface." Jarvis unstrapped and shook his finger in signal. The AT-32 burst up onto the water's surface. The tank transformed, snapping and creaking until it formed into a sleek ship. The door from the control center opened. Heat poured in immediately. Jarvis laughed at the familiar feeling of jungle humidity. Jarvis took the first step toward the deck; already he felt a sense of pride. His team of grunts pulled off something no survey teams, scientists, or explorers had done before.

They survived a whole five minutes on T-13.

The big question was, did their target survive? Was this just a ghost hunt?

Jarvis walked past the armory and up the small staircase onto the deck. The wind was strong, nearly storm-like, but it wasn't cool. Hot wind blew like bad breath. It felt unnatural to Jarvis, who had spent the last two years of relative time crossing the solar system. Fuck Einstein, Jarvis thought, he had no idea how much time had without the pull of gravity. He walked over to the banister on deck and looked down into the water.

The water was clear, and the massive flow of life back and forth was visible to his naked eye. Cooper and Eden stepped on to the deck next. Jarvis looked up at the sky. The clear image of the planet took up the majority of the sky above them. It was close enough that they could make out the shape of Hermea and watch the blue and white storm clouds flow in every direction on the main planet. There was no sun, not like on Earth. Instead, the light came from a star shining on Beta's atmosphere and reflecting back. It was more than bright enough.

Cooper handed Jarvis a pair of sunglasses identical to his. They both laughed as Jarvis put them on. The whole team walked out onto the deck. It never got old; each time they set foot on a new world, or moon. Jarvis let them take in the view for a moment. Jarvis enjoyed looking at the dumbfounded faces. He realized one was missing.

Jarvis looked down the stairs. "Where's Weddle?"

"He's praying," Zana called out.

Jarvis rolled his eyes.

"I suppose we need all the help we can get," Cooper quipped.

Jarvis whistled to alert them, and everyone snapped to attention.

"Let's get some focus here people. This planet is no joke. The sooner we kill this target dead, the sooner we vacate this rock."

CHAPTER 16

THE SHIP FLOATED past a large tree that swayed with the waves. Now that they were past the trees rising out of the water off-shore, they could see a small beach. The mouth of the river was the length of a city block. It looked as if it could swallow a building whole. The trees in the jungle were so thick it was obvious, even from a distance, that barely any light made it to the surface.

They had rarely seen trees like that on Earth. It had been centuries since humans saw any forests or jungles that big. Martian ecologists were the best and had cloned some larger trees, but they were still rare.

"Those are some fucking trees," Strickland said.

Jammer stated the obvious as he dropped a box on to the deck. "Flying drones over that? Not going to see shit."

Jarvis knew no one was going to like giving up his or her drones for the search but that was how they were going to find the target. While the drones weaved in and out of the jungle, the best bet would be to let the AI pilot and the ship's onboard computer do the work. If the data it sent back came across their personal nets, it could overwhelm the user with headaches and nausea. For a warrior to be without a drone was a tough call.

"I know none of you guys are going to like this idea. I'm

sending out my drone to search, I need two other volunteers."
Jarvis scanned the team. Eden and Burnett were already loosening their uniforms.

Eden put up her hand. "Fuck it."

"OK, that's one." Jarvis stopped his eyes on Cason. "And I thought I was with the infamous *Goddamn Killing Machines*. All those colonists afraid of you on Titan and you turds are afraid to be separated from your drones."

Jarvis knew how to push buttons. Cason reached into his case and grabbed his drone. He gave it a little kiss and threw it in the air. He didn't say anything to Jarvis, just looked at Jammer. "It's linked to the main computer. All yours," Cason told the pilot. Jammer nodded his head in acknowledgement.

Cason's drone sped off down the east bank of the river. Within seconds, it had disappeared into the thick of trees. Eden had a new drone, provided by Cooper after Jarvis destroyed her old one. She signaled it to turn on and let the AI take over. The drone accepted its orders and sped to the river's west bank. Jarvis would use his drone in tandem above the river, scanning for human life forms and directing the other two drones.

One by one, the other drones were launched and perched themselves along the deck, ready for action. Burnett dropped on the deck and did ten quick push-ups.

"How's it feel, dawg?" Cason asked.

Burnett got up breathing heavier than ten push-ups should have made him feel. "This gravity is fierce," he answered.

Jarvis laughed and walked past them to the front of the ship. He stood at the railings in front of the giant machine gun turret and cannon. He looked into the darkness under the treetops and thought to himself that this was a fucking hellhole. *Of all the places in the fucking universe, why here?*

The ship rocked on the waves as they entered the mouth of the river. Eden walked up to his side and gripped the railing. "Hey Nick, I've been thinking."

They entered the river. The wind was different once they passed the tree line, calmer. It wasn't quiet. The jungle was a cacophony of sounds; the clicking of insects, chirping of birds, swaying of trees, and howls of creatures big and small filled the sky. It was a symphony of strange life forms that had evolved on this moon over millions of years. Jarvis knew Eden was trying to get his full attention but he couldn't take his eyes off the marvelous sight.

Earth was a dead world, and besides kicking that dead horse, the human species hopped from one engineered rock to another. Jarvis had never seen an environment this natural and full of life that was not Geo-engineered . They used to think the jungles in South America were impressive but they were nothing compared to this.

"What if this is a test?" Eden asked him.

Jarvis shook his head and turned back to Eden. "What?"

"A test. They send us down here to figure out how to survive. Take data on this planet, use us to devise ways to survive. Like lab rats." She waved her hand out to indicate the world in front of them.

"We're here to kill Garay," Jarvis told her.

"He could be dead, we can't trust anything Cooper says." Eden shook her head.

How could Jarvis trust her now? On Earth she was ready to kill him to stay free. There was a time when he was positive she loved him. It took him months to get it through his thick skull that she had wanted to leave with him. None of that really matters now. Everything they knew was three hundred years on the wrong end of a hypersleep trip.

Eden put her hand on his. "Hey, we our fresh out of options, we gotta see this mission through."

Jarvis stepped away but she grabbed on to his arm. "Nick, you can trust me."

He pulled his arm free. "Sure thing." He walked away and went down the steps into the command center.

Cooper and Jammer worked various computers and monitored the drones. Jarvis uploaded the reports. Several points of evidence came together. Residue on the river turned out to be kilotat, a Martian blend of fossil fuel that proved some kind of ship had been there and taken a similar cruise. Cason's drone found a small fleck of dried blood that was months old. They could tell it was human DNA, but it was too damaged to get an identity. The drones continued flying a grid of four-square miles off the bank of the river.

Cooper turned in his chair. "Tell me something, Jarvis; why would someone with your type of training choose this asshole of the universe to hide? Explain to me the psychology of this choice."

Jarvis took one of the command chairs. "Are you admitting that Garay is the target?"

Cooper smiled. "Hypothetically speaking, of course."

"It doesn't take a bio-tech cloner to solve this riddle. Jamal firmly believes that he is the baddest dude in the whole universe." Jarvis lifted his hands and shrugged.

"I'm getting the impression; your whole team certainly believes it," Cooper looked around at the others.

Jarvis nodded in reply.

"He probably believes no one will come for him here." Jarvis pulled up the view from his drone. They watched an outside image on the screen of their ship chugging down the massive river. "The only reason I'd come to this planet is if I thought the whole universe was coming after me."

Cooper studied him in silence for a few seconds. "Why are you really here Jarvis?"

Jarvis felt anger boil inside him. Internally he counted down from ten. Jarvis leaned closer. "Fuck you, you didn't give me a choice."

Cooper grinned. "Don't bullshit me, Jarvis. One by one you brought your team in and now you've dropped them into hell. What I am getting at is you could've stayed hidden, or gone out in a blaze of glory, that is what you types dream about, right?"

Jarvis didn't say a word.

Cooper grinned. "You can bark and talk tough with your squad but your boy *was* your weakness."

Jarvis hated to admit that the smug bastard was right. So he wouldn't admit it, he just keep quiet. Sammy was the first good thing he brought into the universe; every day with his boy, he felt a little redemption. Sammy was sweet, honest, despite the misery around him. When he was with his son, he could forget about the team of killers he trained and unleashed on the solar system.

Then he heard that Cason had killed a Marine on Europa and that Garay and Eden had killed cops. Worst of all, Jamal had slaughtered a SWAT team of UN Rangers. There were monsters out there and he was their Doctor Frankenstein. He had turned them into the death machines they had become. When he looked in the mirror, he told himself that he was doing it for his family, but he knew the reality was something darker than he wanted to admit. He created that monster, and it was his job to kill it.

CHAPTER 17

JARVIS WALKED shirtless onto the deck and stared off into the jungle. The bank of the river was a rocky mess. It hadn't gotten dark yet; it had been three days according to the watch that Jarvis kept on Earth time. It was important to know when you needed to get some sleep or when to eat. It only took a few hours off Earth to realize how much bullshit the concept of time is.

Strickland and Eden kicked a hacky sack around on deck. Burnett sat, as he did every waking hour, at the turret gun. Every three minutes he fired off a burst of rounds. He firmly believed the reason they hadn't been attacked was because of those spent rounds. Burnett studied the jungle edge, and when he got tired or took his eyes off it, his drone picked up the slack. Strickland had complained about trying to sleep while Burnett shot that gun every three minutes. Burnett never responded, it wasn't worth an argument. Cason kept up the firing when Burnett slept.

They had managed to avoid going stir crazy over the seventy-one hours of light. Cason sharpened his long blade and chewed on a toothpick. Weddle remained below reading his Bible. Zana cleaned her rifle, as she had four times since they hit the river. Jarvis held on to the railing and savored the first breeze he had felt on this planet that didn't feel like a hair dryer.

He got a headache watching the planet constantly spin in the sky. Tartarus moved with Beta, but the planet took three Earth days just to spin around. Tartarus was a moon and spun at totally different speed. The sky and shifting clouds on Beta were like a giant computer screen saver. T-13's orbit around Beta took six Earth days, for seventy-two hours they would be plunged into darkness on the far side of the planet from the sun.

Tartarus spun slowly but every three Earth days, they switched from warm to burning hot as their side got the direct light of the sun, opposite of the planet in the sky. It was so bright no one wanted to go on deck, and the deck plates felt like a griddle. They had yet to experience nighttime on Tartarus, which Jarvis preferred to think of as T-13.

This fucking rock didn't have a name when they left Earth.

Every few miles they saw creatures that looked like hippos with camouflage markings. Eden thought they were cute. They turned around and stared at the ship. The computer identified them as hicanus, but they looked fat so they joked about naming them after a CO back at Fort Juno named Carter.

They laughed at them until one of the hicanus jumped out of the water, revealing a mouthful of dagger-like teeth and dragged a sun-basking, dragon-like creature into the river. Burnett shot near the hicanus to scare them off but it hadn't worked. The hicanus kept an eye on them.

Jarvis leaned over the railing and could see the hicanus just below the water line. They were heading down river, swimming beside them like an escort. Jarvis used his neural net to access an underwater camera. Dozen of those hicanus swam just under the hull. They were not afraid of Burnett's gunfire.

Dusk finally approached. The blue and white of Beta's sky faded and the moon's sky grew purple. Jarvis leaned his back against the railing and watched Eden kick the hacky sack.

He had been worried about this. They were sharp when they got here, but now since they made it further than anyone and the planet's wildlife were leaving them alone, everyone but Cason and Burnett were treating this like a vacation. Cooper remained wired to the drones, but the team was getting weak. The sounds of the jungle, which had been ominous, were fading into the background now that night was falling.

Eden missed the sack and looked at Jarvis. "What?"

Jarvis put up his hands and shrugged. "You seem awfully relaxed."

"Can't we just be happy this place is not that dangerous?" asked Strickland.

"Not dangerous?" Burnett laughed. "We haven't stepped off the boat." Burnett never let go of the gun handle. "I'd bet my rations your dumbass hasn't watched one minute of drone telemetry."

Strickland laughed and bounced the hacky sack back into play.

"You should send a drone out to peep on the jurassus," Jarvis waved out at the jungle.

Strickland kept kicking.

"Jurassus?" Eden laughed.

"Yeah. It's body like a gorilla and a head like a T-Rex." Jarvis grinned. "Motherfuckers can climb, use branches like clubs."

Strickland nodded. Burnett turned the large gun up to the sky. "There is some shit up there, and night is coming," Burnett told them.

Jarvis walked towards the back of the ship. He pointed at Burnett. "What he said."

Jarvis sat down on a quiet part of the deck with Zana. He listened to the sound of her towel rubbing oil on her rifle. He looked up at the sky and saw stars. It was the first time he saw them from this planet. He had seen stars from Mars, Europa, and Titan, but this was different. One of those tiny dots of light was the sun. Not just any sun, but that hot-as-hell fucker that burned away in the sky above Earth.

Now he was a few centuries and a billion kilometers removed from that star and actually found himself missing it.

"Eden told me about your son," Zana said to him, not looking up from her weapon.

Jarvis looked back at Zana. She had her rifle relaxed across her lap. Her striking half-African, half-Chinese features were common in the Asian Bloc, but there were not too many like her in the UN colonies. That mix of humans became more common after western Africa joined the Asian Block.

"She doesn't know shit," Jarvis told her.

Zana nodded. "Burnett had a daughter you know, on Europa."

Jarvis raised an eyebrow, surprised that she knew more of Burnett's story.

"Some colonist he nailed," Zana laughed. "He went back when you broke up the band."

"That colonist take him back?" Jarvis asked.

Zana laughed. "Hell no, would you? Surly motherfucker like that. Nah, but give Burnett an ounce of cred, he stuck it out and tried to be a dad."

Jarvis laughed but felt guilty. When he arrested Burnett on Europa he thought it was funny that the hard-boiled soldier had a doll and sippy cup in his shoulder bag. Before Jarvis could get all sappy, he remembered that Burnett also used his drone to try and kill the arrest team and almost took out a public transport in the process. Now it all made sense, his desperation to move things along, to get it done. His anger and frustration when they realized they couldn't go back.

"I told him he needs to let that shit go," said Zana.

Jarvis let her words sink in a second and sat up. He tried not to think about his boy, but it was impossible. He had lost his son and could never get him back. All because he was too stupid to realize they were being tricked. Two hundred and eighty-seven years had slipped through their fingers. He looked at Zana as the light faded away and a line of darkness covered the ship. Jarvis looked up at the sky and back at Zana.

"Yeah, well that's easy for a cold-hearted bitch like you, Zana, you have no idea what it's like to hold a life you created in your hands. It changed everything, all this stuff we've done, all the lives we destroyed. For that time I had with Sammy, it felt like I deserved to be born."

"You done?" Zana listened, but rolled her eyes at him. "You got tricked, and now that boy of yours died hating his father. If he even remembered you. Keep your head in this game. Right here and right now. What have you always told me, *fuck all that regret, it's a trap.*"

Jarvis was about to tell her to mind her own business when a series of screams cut into the sound of the new evening. The howling, chirping, and rustling of trees stopped as the jungle froze. Jarvis watched telemetry from the drones still searching deep in the jungle. The jurassus looked around for a moment, before they took off running. The jungle exploded in chaos.

CHAPTER 18

JARVIS RAN to the edge of the railing and scanned the jungle with night vision goggles. Several of the smaller creatures burrowed into the ground. The whole planet reacted out of fear.

Cooper and Jammer came running up onto the deck. Jarvis walked up to them..

"What the fuck is that?" Zana followed with her rifle

Cooper pointed at the drone above them. "Your drone had been tracking them, it seems to be several thousand of those fucking birds in a tight formation, some kind of migration. They've been following us for forty hours."

"Forty fucking hours?" Asked Jammer

"Yeah, at a distance but they were leaving us alone." Cooper ran a hand through his hair.

"They must hunt at night." Burnett pulled on the large machine gun, locking and loading the weapon.

Jarvis switched his contacts to night vision and zoomed the image. The dragon-birds were coming north toward them at high speeds.

"Arm up boys and girls, those things look hungry," Burnett yelled to them and then laid his head down on the stock of the large rifle. He closed his eyes and Jarvis knew he was playing some kind of electro-thrash song on his neural net. Burnett liked to feel the music in battle. Playing music aloud wasn't the same; you couldn't feel the notes like you could when you played it on your personal net. He had a rhythm in battle and needed his tunes.

Jarvis whistled and directed Cason and Strickland to the front of the ship. Eden protected the command center while Zana and Weddle ran to the flank. Rifles pointed in the air as the chorus of a thousand ear-piercing screams moved towards them.

"Jammer! I need some speed," Jarvis told his pilot.

The ship rocked slightly and water splashed around them as they rocketed down the river. The screams rose in intensity as the swarm got closer. The glass on the command center rattled. Weddle punched the railing and screamed back at the swarm. Burnett turned up the volume of his music; he was the only one not rattled. He was hungry for this.

"Fire as soon as you have a clear line!" Jarvis screamed; he had no idea if he was heard over the cacophony of dragon-birds.

The birds appeared above them. Burnett was the first to open fire, but in seconds, they were all firing. The roar of the machine gun and rifles battled the sound of the screaming birds. Drones launched, diving through the swarm and cutting a path as they spread through the screaming mass. Parts of bodies and whole birds rained down on the deck as the creatures circled at deck level like a hurricane. The ship had become the eye of a nasty storm.

The chaos of the attack was overwhelming. Their bullets were programmed to avoid hitting their own team and they would have been shredded if that programming had failed. The drones were not so lucky; in less than thirty seconds, the signals popped off. Cooper struggled in the command center to find signals as each one disappeared.

"Losing drones!" Cooper yelled over the intercom.

The hull of the ship snapped and banged with bullets and birds. Jarvis received a signal that Cason had stopped firing. Jarvis continued to fire his weapon as he backed toward him.

Cason lay on the deck and screamed as a bird took off with his right hand. Jarvis swung the stock of his rifle around and bashed the bird to the floor of the deck. It spit out Cason's hand as Jarvis crushed the creature. Cason screamed and scooped up his hand with his stump. A bird landed on Cason's chest and took wild bites at his heart. The sound of a thousand rounds firing in every direction mixed in the air with the sound of thousands of carnivorous falsetto screaming birds.

Insanity. The first word that came to mind.

Get below deck! Jarvis gave the command across their net server. He knew they never would've heard his voice. Eden laid down a line of fire while Weddle and Zana made their way to the door. One by one, everyone dropped below deck; only Burnett remained at the turret gun.

Eden held the door open, spraying a line of fire from her automatic pistol. The clip was filled with self-replicating bullets and she had a thousand rounds before she would be dry. She had never thought she would use it all before this moment.

Burnett was covered in blood, screaming and firing in every direction behind the turret. As the swarm attacked, their high-pitched screams only increased in intensity.

Jarvis went to rescue Burnett but Eden held him by his collar.

Burnett spun around, pointing the gun at the door. He pulled the trigger one last time. The rounds tore through the creatures, dropping them to the deck. Burnett jumped onto the deck and slid across the blood-slicked floor. Eden grabbed his legs and pulled him in as Jarvis slammed the door shut.

They all fell down the stairs, hitting the last few as they rolled into the armory. Jarvis looked back at the shut door, but several creatures had followed them below deck. The contained sound of the screams was even worse than out in the open air. Their eardrums rattled. Eden used her handgun to shoot the last four birds flying around the ceiling. Strickland had his hands over his face, screaming. Everyone was bleeding and covered in bites. The thud of dropped rifles was followed by heavy breathing.

"They're like gnats," said Weddle.

"Big fucking ones." Jarvis turned toward a muted scream.

Burnett laid back against the wall, holding one of the smaller bird creatures in his grip. It screamed in anger and desperation as Burnett squeezed the life out of it.

Cooper came out of the command center with a cage. "Don't kill it."

Burnett dropped the bird into a cage. Cooper held it up to his face and laughed. "It's a dragon-bird, probably a hatchling."

"They're gnats if you ask me." Jarvis said looking at the cuts on his arm. He looked around the room. Cason screamed in pain in one corner. Zana grabbed a med kit and sat down next to him. She put on a glove and moved his shirt to look at the wound in his chest. It was large and poured blood on the floor.

Weddle grabbed the second med kit. He started sealing Cason's wounds with the skin-binder and assuring the man it would be OK. The dragon-bird in the cage continued to scream. Strickland jumped up and pointed his pistol at the cage. Cooper stood in front of him. "We need to study it."

Strickland stared at Cooper, blood and sweat rolling down his forehead. "Then get the thing to shut the fuck up!"

The ship rocked. They heard a deep howl-like sound under the surface of the water. They heard a horrible noise, like several dozen fingernails scratching on chalkboards. Under the hull dozens of claws scraped metal. Cooper and Jarvis looked at each other before going into the command center.

Jammer spun his chair and shook his head at them. "This is all kinds of fucked up."

Cooper pulled up the image beamed from the drone a mile above them. They couldn't even see the ship, it was covered with the dragon-birds. Cooper switched to the deck camera; it was a blur of swirling dragon-birds. Jarvis grunted at the insanity of it. Jammer zoomed in the camera.

"Check this," he told them.

The camera zeroed in on Cason's hand. What was left of it. Some of Cason's blood remained on the deck and it slowly mixed with the dragon-bird blood. All of the blood seeped down the sides of the ship and into the water.

Cooper switched to the underwater camera. "Oh shit," he murmured.

The hicanus were swimming incredibly fast under the ship despite their size. Two dozen or more were reaching and biting on the metal hull. The blood was driving them mad.

"You think those hicanus are attracted to the blood?" asked Jammer.

Jarvis nodded. "I think that's pretty fucking clear."

Eden walked in the command center, sweating buckets. Weddle had sealed her cuts.

"What the fuck is down there?" she asked them.

"Hicanus." Jarvis grinned. "A whole posse."

"Those fat ass things?" Eden scoffed.

"They're big, but move pretty fast," said Jammer.

The noise of the screaming dragon-birds above and the scratching hicanus below was like a horrid symphony. They had to get away from those things. Jarvis pulled up Cason's drone telemetry. The forest here was thick, trees so close to together it would be hard to travel on land. They couldn't stay here and they couldn't go up on deck.

Jarvis pointed back at the armory. "Eden, get everyone strapped in."

Eden shook her head. "What are we doing?"

Jarvis grabbed Jammer and pulled him away from the helm. "Strap up Jammer."

Jammer was going to argue, but Jarvis had already strapped himself into the pilot's chair. Cooper put on the straps at the co-pilot seat.

"I hope you have a plan," Cooper said to him.

"We need to get those fuckin' gnats off us." Jarvis pushed buttons on the control panel and cued the AT's computer with his net. He signaled all hands across their servers.

Prepare to shift to land mode. Strap in!

Jarvis gunned the engine. The ship took off through the river even faster; this time he turned the boat for the shoreline. The rest of the squad scrambled to get into their seats and lock down.

"We need to go faster if you are going to catch enough air." Cooper pointed out what Jarvis already knew. The ship hit the beachhead going one hundred miles per hour. The large ship bounced off the rocky shore into the air. Jarvis sent the computer the password and code that triggered the change. In mid-air the pieces of the ship moved, shifting and popping into position. Several of the dragon-birds were caught and crushed as the ship became a solid tank. The last piece locked into place with the front turret gun leading the way.

The tank hit the ground and the treads pushed them at high velocity into the first line of trees. The dragon-birds flew into the trees while still trying to attack their prey, now a massive land tank. Jarvis assumed they were born with an instinct to keep attacking until their prey had submitted. From the drone footage he had seen, the adult dragon-birds rarely gave up. The tank burst into trees as thick as buses and shredded them; the towering giants fell in their wake.

A group of jurassus jumped from tree to tree, screaming at the tank while it battled its way through the forest. Pieces of lumber and a thick downpour of splinters rained behind them. The dragon-birds screamed louder; several choked on the debris. It was impossible for them to follow in the chaos.

Inside the tank, everyone shook like an escape pod falling in orbit. Every few seconds they hit a tree and it boomed, rattling their bones. Jarvis watched from Cason's drone as the dragon-birds turned back to the river. He hit the brakes, his feet straining as they pushed the pedal hard into the floor. They stopped just as they pounded into another massive tree.

It was quiet after the initial blast. The tree in front of them still stood.

"Holy shit." Cooper tried to catch his breath. "You crazy fucker."

The tree in front of them whistled as it finally fell away from them. Jarvis and Cooper both closed their eyes. The ground shook under the tank with the thunderous boom.

A chorus of curses came from the team strapped in the armory. Jarvis unhooked himself and ran back. He saw Eden wide-eyed in her straps. He scanned everyone. No one seemed hurt, except Cason. His head dipped down and his body was lifeless in the straps. He had annoyed Jarvis with his attitude the last few days, but Jarvis didn't want to see him dead.

"Shit," he muttered under his breath.

"That got rid of the hatchlings..." Cooper spoke as he walked in the room. He stopped when he saw Cason.

He hurried over to the injured man and lifted up his head. Zana was next to him, trying to look strong. She was hurt and angry. Weddle unhooked himself and went straight to his knees muttering some kind of mantra. Cooper lifted up Cason's head.

The eyes looked strange. Frozen open. Cooper scanned the members of the team.

"How did this man die?" He demanded.

No one felt like answering.

Zana cleared her throat. "Those fucking gnat things, they took his hand. He was bleeding."

Cooper unhooked Cason's body and lifted it over his shoulder. "Clear the room. I need to do an autopsy."

More than one person gasped. Jarvis snapped his fingers. "Cool it, give the man some room. We'll meet in the galley, get some rations and cool off."

Cooper laid Cason's body on the table. The dragon-bird in the cage had stopped screaming. It watched Cooper as he took a knife and cut off Cason's shirt. Everyone left until Jarvis was alone, staring at Cooper.

"I would like some privacy. I think you and the team should

make a plan for getting back to the river. We still have a target to track." Cooper didn't look back at him.

Jarvis was beginning to think it was impossible for any one person to survive this world. They were risking their lives on a wild goose chase.

"We've been here three days. We haven't seen shit," Jarvis remarked.

Cooper lifted Cason's eyelids and stared into the man's dead eyes. "Colonel Jarvis you really need let go of Earth concepts of time. This is a long river; you need to give this search more effort. We have seen fuel traces and human DNA fragments; the target is here."

"Is that right?" Jarvis was doubtful.

Cooper dropped his knife with a clank on the table. He looked up at Jarvis with barely contained rage. "I need to make sure some toxin didn't kill him in his weakened state that could affect us. This is a mission priority. I'm going to look for weaknesses on the hatchling too."

"Gnat, we'll call it a gnat," Jarvis sneered.

Cooper rolled his eyes. Jarvis wanted to smack him, but maybe it was time he tried to figure out this jungle that surrounded them. Jarvis turned to leave the room and was pulling the door shut when Cooper ordered him, "Get us back to the river, Colonel."

Jarvis slammed the door.

CHAPTER 19

THE AIR outside the AT-32 was hot, humid, and moist. Jarvis popped the hatch on his air tank and heard a popping sound as the seal broke and the Earth-style oxygen escaped. Jarvis breathed the native air into his lungs through the mask for the first time; it was a long and deep breath. The oxygen was rich different from the actual air on Earth, which felt stale in comparison. It was hard for Jarvis to describe; it just felt different. Jarvis, Burnett, and Eden were under a thick cover of trees on the far side of the giant planet, away from any light source. It was darker than a cave.

Burnett crawled out behind him and switched on the light at the end of his rifle. Both men jumped when they saw the jurassus hanging upside down from a branch fifteen feet away. Burnett fired but Jarvis knocked his rifle up, making the bullets burst into the tree above the animal. The jurassus took off screaming.

"Way to greet our new neighbors." Eden laughed as she pulled herself up.

Jarvis and Eden both flipped their rifle lights on. Several species of large animals scattered as the lights joined Burnett's. Eden turned hers to shine behind them, and laughed. They had cleared an ugly path back through the jungle. In the distance, you could hear the roaring of the river. Slowly the sounds of the night in the jungle faded, as if the jungle was holding its collective breath and then releasing. Jarvis felt an uncomfortable feeling, as if the entire jungle watched them crawl out of the tank.

The drone held its position, watching the gnats who waited for them to return to the river. They swarmed at the beach, spinning like hurricane winds. Jarvis was staring at the footage through his neural net when it blinked out. A few seconds later, they heard the roar of a dragon-bird in the sky. Jarvis smacked the top of his rifle in frustration.

"We're lucky the drone lasted that long," said Eden.

The dragon-bird was likely to spit out the drone when it realized it wasn't food.

"Only two drones left," said Burnett.

Jarvis didn't have time to count. He knew the battle with those dragon-birds was destructive, but he didn't know it had decimated their drones.

"So we're tracking old school," Jarvis told them.

They heard a tree bending, almost breaking behind them. They turned their lights around. Several jurassus raced down the length of the fallen tree toward them. Jarvis fired several rounds in front of their feet and signaled to his team.

"I've seen enough." He was the last one in and sealed the hatch.

Eden watched Jarvis seal the hatch. He paused at the door. A few seconds of silence, and then the roar. It sounded like a dozen heavy feet dancing on top of the hull. The sound was overwhelming, but despite the bombardment, Eden tried to center herself. She dropped her rifle and thought about Cason. He had survived so much.

Eden spun slowly, looking for Cason's body. A trail of blood stained the floor toward the armory door. Eden crouched down and stared at the dried blood.

Jarvis signaled to the command center. "Jammer, back up. All the way to the river."

Burnett walked back to the galley; Eden looked up from the blood and stared at the armory door. She felt Jarvis looking at her.

Jarvis spoke in a commanding tone. "Hey everybody, get some rations."

Eden ignored him. How could she eat at a moment like this? She headed toward the armory door.

"Eden, let Cooper do his..."

Eden opened the door and Cooper looked up. He leaned over the table but she could see he had the dragon-bird pinned to the table next to Cason's body. Cason's chest was cracked open, his rib cage visible. The dragon-bird screamed once on the table and Cooper relaxed again. He straightened his blood-covered white coat.

"I asked for some privacy," Cooper told her.

Jarvis followed Eden and grabbed her arm. She pulled away. She walked closer to the table and looked at the bloody stump that had been Cason's arm.

"I've been thinking about Cason." She said quietly.

Cooper didn't say anything; just looked at her.

"What do you know about our mission in Taiwan?" Her eyes lifted to Cooper's.

Cooper looked over her shoulder at Jarvis. "I don't have time for this."

Eden stepped closer until she was in Cooper's face. "You said you read our files. What did it say about Taiwan? Your bosses gave us the credits for that one so I won't believe you didn't download the intel."

Cooper looked straight at Eden. "We don't have time for this."

Jarvis stepped into the room and slid the door closed. "Oh, I think we can spare a minute."

Cooper kept his eyes locked on Eden, not blinking. "Details are fuzzy. It was a highly classified assassination, neither powers would admit to it, and you took heavy fire on the extraction."

"Heavy fire," Eden laughed. "It was a certified shit-storm."

Cooper looked at Jarvis who nodded.

"Thing of beauty," Jarvis grinned. "If blood and guts is your thing."

Eden's eyes tightened a little. "You see, when we got on the jumper that night, Cason must have taken about eight bullets and he lost a good chunk of his natural leg. He hurt like hell the next day, but he was one tough motherfucker. So you pardon me if I find it strange that he bled to death after losing his fucking hand."

Cooper looked around the room nervously. The question seemed to surprise him. Jarvis took another step forward, throwing him a bone. "Did you find a neurotoxin?"

Cooper looked down at Cason's body.

"Not yet, but I think it's possible that if there was one, we'd all be dead." Cooper sounded resigned.

Eden didn't think it was possible for Jarvis to believe this. She glanced and him and then locked her eyes back on Cooper. "He wouldn't die that easy."

Cooper looked at her; confidence filled him like a balloon taking on air. He took a step back and pointed at the sheet covering Cason's body. "Then how do you explain the body on the table."

Eden couldn't explain it. "I'm asking you."

Jarvis studied her confusion for a moment and stepped in between them.

"Eden, get back to the command center. Make sure Jammer gets us back to the river."

Eden looked at Jarvis, their eyes locking only for a moment. She shook her head and walked out. When the door shut her behind her, she let out a deep breath. Eden stared at the door and thought about Nick Jarvis. He had changed. Something was different. She assumed it was his six years of domestic life but for the first time ever she didn't feel safe under his command.

CHAPTER 20

IT WAS EASIER to shift modes in mid-air. It only took a few seconds and they crashed into the river as a ship. Burnett opened the door to the deck and fired a blast of automatic rounds, knocking the dragon-birds back. He pumped the rocket launcher at the bottom of his rifle barrel. The rocket sailed into the air crowded with dragon-birds and exploded into an invisible gas. They couldn't hear the explosion over the screams of the retreating creatures. The dust from the gas settled on the deck, and would repel them for a few hours, and then they would have to repeat the process.

Jarvis was the first to step out on deck and almost slipped on fresh blood. Cason's hand was gone, having been devoured by the dragon-birds. Blood puddled on the deck. It looked like human blood but he knew it was alien.

"Who wants to clean up this mess?" He threw the question out to the whole team.

Strickland was first to grab a hose and sprayed down the deck. Jarvis looked up but the star-filled sky was impossible to see beyond the swarming dragon-birds. The older dragon-birds were a bit higher, also circling. At least a hundred of the nasty things, just waiting to make dinner of them.

Cooper walked on to the deck. "Is it working?

Jarvis thought it was obvious. Something was repelling the creatures for now. "It seems like it."

"Is the gas toxic to us?" Cooper seemed worried.

Jarvis shrugged. "It's your armory."

Cooper pointed at Burnett. "Fire one of those rockets every hour."

Burnett mockingly saluted and Strickland laughed with him.

Jarvis walked to the edge of the deck and closed his eyes as a gust of warm wind blew down the river. Despite the warm bursts of wind, the night was growing colder quickly. Jarvis also realized this was the first time he walked on deck and didn't feel the uncomfortable pull of the higher gravity. His legs felt stronger; Cooper had told them that would happen.

Jarvis opened his eyes when he heard a thump on the deck. "What the fuck are you doing?" Weddle had fallen to his knees and had his hands out.

Weddle ignored him and placed his Bible pad on the deck. The reader came to life and the light of the screen shined lit up his face. Jarvis never understood traditional religious freaks. As the human race left the boundaries of Earth and technology progressed to the point where no miracle was out of reach, who the fuck needed some tired old god? People in this century who think the human race are special or in the image of some divine power are rare.

"Yea, though we walk through the valley in the shadow of death," Weddle droned on as Jarvis walked off. Weddle's voice suddenly sounded normal, as if his sanity returned. "We're in Hell, Jarvis."

It was strange hearing Weddle sound like his old friend again. Jarvis turned to look at Weddle, down on his knees. He knew what Weddle meant. Even at night the air was hot and the screaming predators never stopped their screeching. The rad-pills only did so much when the massive planet filling the day sky sent wave after wave of radiation. He silently agreed with

Weddle's assessment but he couldn't have his team thinking that way.

"Nothing new about it, son. Marching into Hell to kill demons is what people pay us for."

Jarvis walked below deck and fell asleep as soon as his body hit the rack.

He woke from a nightmare he couldn't recall. . His feet hit the cold floor and the dragon-bird screams shook his eardrums. He heard the never-ending scratching of the hicanus under the ship. You couldn't escape the sounds. He stumbled to the bathroom and aimed for the small toilet. He didn't have a clue how long he had slept but he didn't feel refreshed or fully awake when he walked into the galley.

Zana and Eden sat at a table talking. Eden held Zana's hand. The conversation came to a halt when he walked in, but there was no silence. The hicanus kept scratching under the hull. It seemed louder than before.

"Am I interrupting something?" Jarvis asked.

"No," they both said.

Jarvis grabbed a pack of rations and tore it open as he sat. It was hard to eat, or think for that matter, with those things scratching at the hull. None of them spoke. Jarvis forked the protein-formulated rations into his mouth. He was about to ask them what their fucking problem was when Jammer came into the room.

He stomped on the floor as if he could scare the hicanus off and sat down across from Jarvis. He had bags under his eyes and his brown skin looked pale. Jarvis tried to sound positive. "I know it's going to be rough sleeping with this noise, but try and get some rack time."

Jammer tore open a ration package with his teeth and he squeezed out a bite. He responded with a mouthful of protein. "It's about to get worse."

Jarvis looked confused. Then something in the prep file came back to him. "Moon rain?"

"Buckle up!" Jammer yelled at the crew.

The rings of Beta looked like floating rocks in the sky. They didn't look big the surface of Tartarus, but Jarvis knew they were as big as buses. Beyond the rings an impossible number of stars stared back at him.

Cooper walked on the deck. "This is not going to be pretty."

The rings developed a few thousand years ago, when humans were still fighting crusades in the Middle East. A moon fell into the orbit of the gas giant and exploded. Most of the moon burned off in the planet's volatile atmosphere. What wasn't destroyed continued to orbit the planet in these rings. This meant every ninety hours in orbit, the atmosphere around Tartarus's northern hemisphere crossed path with the rings.

Jarvis kept his neck craned to watch the unmoving stars. It was several minutes before he saw the first red flare streak across the sky. The dragon-birds screeched as they flew away from the danger. A second flare stretched for miles and gave the horizon a red glow. A third exploded with thunderous boom, hundreds of miles away but enough to rattle them.

"It's beautiful," Eden whispered.

It was hard to take your eyes off the sky. Jarvis wanted to marvel at it but he knew the moon they were on was heading for this storm. A few heartbeats later the entire sky went crimson and the whistle of space debris broke through the veil of night.

"Everyone below deck now!" Cooper shouted.

Burnett had dozed off in the turret gun chair; he woke violently to the barked command. He looked over as Jarvis tugged on his shirt. A fireball sped through the sky while several others burned up into dust high above them. For every ten that burned up, at least one fireball rained down, blasting into the jungle and dragging through it in flames.

Jarvis shut the hatch once everyone was inside. The planet shook, but under the water the hicanus kept wasting their time trying to get into the bottom of the ship. Cooper directed the two remaining drones higher into the sky. The dragon-birds must have submerged themselves in the ocean to hide from the falling moon chunks. The drones kept moving to avoid being hit. The sky suddenly burned into an orange midnight, as if raining flares. The fireballs that made it to the ground burst through the trees and exploded against the soil.

Tartarus shook and the walls of the ship rattled as the monster thunderstorm passed over. It continued for thirty minutes and the ship warmed as the jungle exploded into flames on both sides of the river. Even locked into the ship going down the river they could hear the screams of a thousand creatures burning.

Jarvis looked at Weddle. *Maybe he had a point.*

CHAPTER 21

JARVIS COULDN'T WATCH the video feed anymore. It was amazing they had not died. He knew what a nuke attack sounded and felt like. They had just survived an hour of that feeling repeatedly. As it faded away the group relaxed.

The night filled with new sounds such as the roar of vast fires and screams from the dying creatures.

Cooper sent the drones up ahead; the sky above them was a wall of smoke. They couldn't see a damn thing on camera. Jammer and Cooper stared at the screens, willing an image to form. The only camera still giving them a signal was the one under the boat which sent back image after image of the hicanus swimming after them. They didn't need a camera to tell them that. Those fat hippo-looking things never stopped scratching the hull.

The fans didn't keep the heat down and Jarvis had to stand right in front of them to feel any relief. The outer walls felt like heating coils in an oven. Every member of the team except Weddle came in at least once to try to find out what was happening. Jarvis wiped sweat away every few seconds and felt light-headed.

To himself, he cursed this stupid fucking moon. He went over all his decisions that got them into this ordeal. He had been so afraid of a trial, of his team having their crimes listed in public, all because they had finally pushed the wrong button. The real problem is that he knew they would lose. They couldn't deny being monsters, that's what made them rich. They were professional monsters who kept the system going. When you do the dirty work, wrapping yourself in a flag doesn't save your ass. The symbols on that flag matter less than the credits in the account. The fact is that they found him. He was forced to bring in the whole team before the ones they could catch on their own would go to trial and end up on ICE.

Before Sammy, he would have told them to fuck off. He would have died fighting. He had tried not to think about Sammy and Melissa. He knew they died hating him, but he wanted badly to know what happened to them. He hoped they lived a peaceful, normal life. As he went down this river rolling through a burning hell light years from his son's world, he had to admit it to himself: they used his son and he was dumb enough to fall for it.

Eden knocked on the wall. It was her third time looking in on them. "How bad is it?"

Jammer shook his head. Jarvis plopped down in a chair. Eden came into the room and leaned against the wall. He felt guilt looking at her - even now. Missing his boy, but happy to be here with Eden.

"Well?"

"Uh...Not sure but I think a forest the size of Brazil is burning down," Jammer explained. *And were in the middle of it.*

"Great. Got to hand it to you Jarvis, you have a knack for finding the worst hellholes in the universe." Eden said.

Jarvis studied her face. She was pissed; she only called him by his last name when she was angry. He didn't blame her. The information in the file was spotty but if reports were correct the moon rain usually hit the north ocean, now that it hit the forest, they had a potential blackout of light that could last weeks in Earth time, like a mini-nuclear winter.

"Just what we need. A blackout," Jammer said, leaning back.

"No." Cooper pulled up a picture of the night side of Tartarus and the image zoomed in so they could see the smoke billowing out. Cooper sped up the image a bit. "I got a good image from the drop ship, twenty minutes ago. So there's no blackout. At least not completely."

Another huge block of clouds crossed the daylight terminator that slowly moved toward the 'you are here' dot moving up the river.

Cooper shook his head. "Look at the projections! That is one major storm and that fucker will hit this area in half an hour, hurricane strength."

Eden bent down and smacked the side of the monitor. "Bullshit, I'm getting a look." She turned toward the hatch.

"Wait, it's my command, I'll look." Jarvis followed her but turned back to Jammer. "Full speed, get us out ahead of the storm. It may put out the fire but its going to kill us in the process."

Jarvis stopped in the hallway. It was the first moment they had been alone together since landing on Tartarus. They both paused and he looked into her eyes, just long enough for her to smile a little. He felt a weight lift off his shoulders. *Maybe she wasn't mad at all.*

"What are you doing?" Eden asked.

Jarvis reached up to spin the wheel to open the latch and had to pull his hand back. His fingertips burned a soft red while the handle burned hot. Jarvis used the corner of his uniform to turn it, and sweat poured down his face again. The rush of heat and smoke pushed its way through the crack in the hatch. Jarvis snapped his fingers at an environmental mask hanging on the wall. Eden threw it to him and grabbed her own.

As they stepped out on the deck, Eden pulled the hatch shut. It was as if they had walked into Dante's nightmares. It was hard to imagine a hell that was worse than the one on each side of the river. Miles of trees stretching into the sky burned like candlewicks. The black smoke carried the smell of burning creatures that couldn't burrow underground. The dancing orange light of the fire lit Eden's face and revealed her shock at the extent of the damage.

The crackling sound of burning wood had replaced the unending clicking of the arm-sized insects that inhabited the jungle. Steam rose off the water as the river slowed and nearly boiled.

"If the target was out there, he's gone now," said Eden.

Jarvis ignored her and scanned the forest, taking in the destruction. It was impossible to tell if a storm was coming but the map said the storm was rolling out of the south ocean. It would come from their west across the long part of the land mass. Jarvis put his hand in the air and felt a slight breeze coming from the west.

"Jarvis?" The radio crackled inside their masks.

Cooper forwarded a drone stream to his neural net. Sent from his personal drone, the video stream showed his drone was beyond the fires, and according to the signal only 220 kilometers to the north. The jungle faded with the fire and he realized the land changed into a desert. A short band of dry land sat at the moon's equator, a signal they had made almost half the journey up the red river of Tartarus.

The desert was not as barren as its Earth counterparts with several scattered islands of palm tree-like foliage.

"Are you watching?" Cooper's voice boomed through his mask.

"Yes." Jarvis replied.

Eden turned to look at Jarvis, pointing at her temple to indicate she wanted to see the footage. He linked her up and they watched the video, which was crystal clear in three dimensions inside his net browser. A row of about fifteen crosses lined up in the desert and six jurassus were nailed to them in a grotesque mockery of the crucifixion. They had been gutted and were teeming with giant insects. One creature looked like a praying mantis the size of Rottweiler and it chewed aggressively at a pile of jurassus guts. They were scarecrows; Garay had used this tactic before, it was to scare away more jurassus from attacking.

"Jesus," Eden whispered.

"Not really," replied Jarvis.

Beyond the mutilated bodies, there was a camp with tents stretching out across the desert. The drone lifted up above it; a dozen tents and a hastily constructed shelter made from the remains of an old riverboat sat in the middle of the desert. It looked exactly like a ship they had used back in the old solar system.

"Flooding could have stranded the ship out there." Cooper said into the mask.

Jarvis didn't wait for Eden; he ran back to the hatch. His mask was off and he was in the command center in thirty seconds. Eden was right behind him. Jarvis snapped his fingers at Jammer to let him in the seat.

"Life signs?" Jarvis asked.

Jammer shook his head. Cooper spun in his chair. "Somebody was there."

Jarvis took command of his drone and flew it down into the camp. It buzzed quickly through the improvised village.

"You seeing what I'm seeing?" Jarvis asked the rest of them.

Eden didn't answer, but leaned down over his shoulder to get a better look at the screen. That camp at one time had more than just one person.

"There is no proof it is him." Eden shook her head.

"Well, if it's Garay, he's not alone," Burnett said from the door to the command center. Eden and Jarvis turned to acknowledge him.

"We can't underestimate them, whoever they are." Jarvis took a deep breath. "They've already lived longer than any other known expeditions."

"Garay doesn't ride with lightweights," Burnett said as he turned and left the command center.

The drone kept moving toward the crashed ship. It was an older all-terrain multi-mode vessel, like the one they were aboard. It looked very much like the ship they used back on Earth called *The Venture*. Its hull was cracked and it looked as if a dragon-bird had taken a bite out of it. Its front end had smashed from hitting the sand at high speed. Without saying it aloud, they all knew what happened.

This ship was attacked when it flew into the atmosphere. Perhaps the crew didn't know the dragon-birds were blind and hunted by sensing the motion of flight. They managed to escape - barely crashing here in the desert. Something killed them, or ran them off, but not before they had rebuilt the exterior to make it into a shelter. The drone spun around the outside of the hull and Jarvis found himself holding his breath. Then he saw what he was afraid to see.

The Venture.

Jarvis spun in his chair to stare at Jammer. The ship was registered in Jammer's name, it was considered his ship. Jammer shook his head.

"Jammer you were supposed to trash that fucking ship on Titan," Jarvis yelled.

Jammer looked away. "I know."

Eden whistled. "Way to go Jams, that fucking ship is loaded with shit we don't want the government, any fucking government, to see."

Jammer shook his head and wagged his finger. "It's a good ship, I just couldn't trash it. It doesn't matter, that was hundreds of years ago, if you think about it."

"Really, Jammer? Since when are you a legal expert on the statute of limitations and relative time dilation?" Jarvis slammed his fist on the counter.

Jammer ignored his question and pointed at the screen. "It's Garay, no doubt that motherfucker is here. He knew, he helped me stash the ship."

"Doesn't explain how it got four light years from where you hid it?" Eden shook her head.

Jarvis ignored Jammer and looked at Eden. He raised an

eyebrow. Eden shook her head and whispered. "Bullshit, Garay went to sleep with the rest of us."

He walked out of the command center. Jarvis closed his eyes and listened to the scratching at the bottom of the ship. He was here, and Jarvis knew that even if no one else survived, Garay was still their target.

CHAPTER 22

EDEN SAW the pain on his face. Jarvis should've been wearing something to help him breath. He should have been sleeping, the ship kept chugging down the river hour after hour into the long night. The air had become thick with soot. The ship bounced along the river like a skipping stone going full speed. You couldn't see the forest, just two solid columns of flame on each shore. The smoke hit her mask and the wind blew her hair back, tangling in the rifle slung across her back. The deck had a surreal orange glow.

She held a breathing mask up for him. "Nick, take it please."

He was slow to except it. She wondered how long he was planning to breathe the toxic air.

"You feeling sorry for yourself?" She waggled the mask in his face.

"Fuck you." He took the mask but didn't put it on.

She had always been there for him, and she was never sure he respected how much did for him or the times she saved him.

"We can't lose you, and I need your focus," She snapped.

He placed the straps over his head but kept his eyes down-river. What they could see of the jungle was gone, like an eraser wiping away a drawing. If the sky hadn't been filled with burning trees, they would be able to see the purple light of dawn. All they heard was the sound of flames eating away at the jungle. An occasional scream cut through the noise and each pained shriek sent shivers down Eden's spine despite the oven-like heat. Creatures large and small dove into the river as the ship sped along. The hicanus were finally diverted from their incessant scratching at the bottom of the ship; they turned now to feed on the animals jumping into the river. Although at intervals, they could hear one or two hicanus continuing to scratch away.

Jarvis pointed to the sky ahead. "Cooper says the storm is catching up to us."

Eden felt a single drop of water hit her hand. She held it up and the single drop rolled down like a tear across her palm. It was not Earth water, it felt thicker, not quite syrup-like, but different. She looked up and a drop of water hit her mask. A third drop on her shoulder.

"You feel that?" Eden's voice was muffled by the mask.

They heard a far off rumble of thunder, high pitched screams cut through the jungle. Jarvis raised his hand. The wind came from the west, stronger now. Eden gripped the railing. The wind continued to strengthen.

"I think the storm is here," she said.

Eden pulled on his arm, but Jarvis didn't say anything, just watched the sky churn. The wind swirled the smoke like burnt cotton candy. A gust of strong wind knocked Jarvis onto the deck. His M-25 rifle slammed into his back and Eden fell on top of him. Her rifle slammed into his gut and knocked his breath away. Eden never saw anything like this storm on Earth or any of the colonies.

The storm clouds sped across the sky, pushing the colossal plumes of smoke into its swirl. Within seconds, the sky opened up with a downpour the Earth hadn't seen in hundreds of years. It came so fast both Eden and Jarvis lost their masks. They spit and coughed up water. The river rolled under intense waves and they rolled across the slick deck.

Eden grabbed on to the railing and pulled herself up. Jarvis hung onto the soaking wet socks at her ankles and held on for his life.

"Jarvis!" Jammer screamed through the intercom.

Jarvis couldn't form words against the force of the storm. Eden watched him struggle to speak before text appeared in her neural net.

Fucking shitstorm out here! We need help getting below deck.

It felt like being under water. She could feel the ship rocking under them. The wind blew the rain in every direction. Eden had one arm wrapped around the railing and another holding Jarvis's shirt. She pulled him with her toward the light of the hatch, which was close. The hatch opened and Jarvis managed to steady himself on the deck and shove Eden toward it.

"Fuck!" Jarvis spat out more water. "That came quick."

Strickland helped pull them inside. Eden looked back out to the river's west shore. Trees danced wildly against the wind, but the flames were dying. Even the burning embers on the jungle floor were losing their glow.

Eden and Jarvis fell into the room. Strickland twisted the hatch door shut and laughed nervously, they were soaked. Eden and Jarvis lay on the floor and Eden had her arms around Jarvis, clutching on to him. They were both breathing intensely. Strickland laughed again but they could barely hear him over the howl of the wind outside. Jarvis and Eden were not amused.

Strickland stopped laughing and cleared his throat. "Yeah, I'll uh, look for a clean towel."

He left and Jarvis relaxed his sopping wet body into her arms. Eden didn't let go; she thought for sure that he was going slide off the ship up there. For years, she had told herself not to forgive him. To forget him. But now, across centuries and light years, everything had changed.

"Thank you," Jarvis said. Just two words but they sounded different. He sounded like he meant it. Eden nodded, resting her face in his wet hair. She had been a warrior for so long she never let herself feel the raw comfort of touch. The warmth coming off him was enough for a few moments to erase the hell beyond the walls. Jarvis closed his eyes; she knew he was feeling the same relief. Jarvis tried to get up but Eden held him in place. She felt her breath catching on his ear, his skin so close.

"I can't lose you," he whispered.

A part of her wanted to scream—*then why did you leave me?* She held it in as they heard Strickland return. She gently kissed his ear.

"Not again." His voice so low she barely heard it.

Eden let go. Jarvis stood up before Strickland walked in. The ship rocked hard again. They all fell over. The ship's metal ached and bent under the force of the wind. Strickland helped Jarvis up first before offering Eden a hand. They all fought to keep standing as the ship rocked.

Strickland looked Jarvis in the eyes. "Hey colonel, fuck this planet."

Eden nodded.

CHAPTER 23

BURNETT FIRED a rocket that woke Jarvis up. He had fallen asleep on the deck with his uniform top balled under his head. The dragon-birds had closed in around the ship but reared back, screaming high-pitched wails as the gas dispersed. It hung around the deck and Jarvis didn't want to think about what garbage they were breathing in. Their lungs had evolved on a different world to breathe different air. He couldn't think too much about it or he would get itchy.

Eden sat in front of him, her legs dangling through the railings, forehead pressed against the metal and her eyes closed. The warm breeze blew through her hair.

Not long after the storm passed, what was left of the jungle thinned out and now they could see for miles across rolling sand dunes. They went from an intense, humid heat to holy-fucking-shit dry heat in a matter of minutes. Covered in sweat, Jarvis wanted to jump in the river. He knew it was too dangerous though. It was torture, rolling for days down a river you didn't feel safe jumping in.

Jarvis shook his head and the dream came back to him. It didn't have the foggy surreal quality of most dreams. It played out just as he remembered it. Burnett sat at the back of the room, faking tears, trying to look scared. Jarvis saw through him like a pane of freshly cleaned glass.

Burnett watched the dragon-birds disperse and relaxed, laying the warm rifle across his lap. He sat on the turret gun's chair sides and propped his legs on the railings. Jarvis walked towards him and considered the dream. No matter how far they traveled together across space and time and here they were back at the same problem.

"I was just thinking about the day we recruited you and Garay."

Burnett kept his eyes out overlooking the dessert. He ignored Jarvis.

"He got us into trouble again."

Burnett stood up. He looked down at Jarvis.

"I'm gonna see this through, I won't hesitate. If I get the chance I'll kill him, but know one thing, Jarvis."

Jarvis lifted an eyebrow. Burnett bumped his shoulder as he passed.

"When this is over I have half a mind to drop you next."

Jarvis thought about Melissa and Sammy and it hurt him again. He knew Burnett had knives twisting in his heart. Jarvis grabbed his shoulder. "I lost my family too."

Burnett locked eyes with him. Jarvis could see the hurt and anger doing battle within him. Burnett stepped slowly back. No more words needed to be said.

Jarvis went back to the command center. Cooper and Jammer had the door shut and the A/C blasting. It didn't do anything. The air blew in cold but you had to sit on the vent to feel anything but heat.

Cooper spun in his chair. "What are you doing?"

"Checking in," Jarvis replied.

Jammer pushed buttons and the engine began to cool down.

Cooper pointed back at the door. "We just hit the landing zone. Suit up."

Jarvis cursed and slid the door back open. He walked into the armory and stopped in his tracks. Zana sat stoically at the table where Cason's dead body was wrapped and tagged. She had her rifle across her lap.

Jarvis pointed behind her. "I gotta suit up."

Zana ignored him and Jarvis walked around her to grab his gear. He thought about saying something, anything. Frankly he was confused as to why Zana was so beat up about Cason.

He cleared his throat. "We found the camp; we're going on shore."

Zana nodded, but he didn't think she heard him. He was about to order her to suit up but thought better of it. Jarvis grabbed his suit by the nylon legs and pulled them over his uniform, attaching the armor jacket and sealing it with a snap. He was contained in the flexible armor and felt the cooling system bring his temperature down. The suit increased his strength and speed and was designed to operate for a minute even after his heart stopped. They only had three in the AT.

Jarvis grabbed an extra self-replicating clip for his rifle although it was doubtful he would ever need more than 2,000 rounds. He lifted his rifle and walked up to the deck with his helmet under his arm.

"Suit up, boys and girls. Next two into armor wins a prize."

Strickland dropped his cards on the deck; it was a useless winning hand. "Somehow, I doubt that."

The ship shook as it rammed into the sandy beach. Jarvis walked to the railings and put on his helmet. The helmet morphed to his head and became invisible over his features. He looked at the sand; his visor transmitted a signal to his neural net and magnified the image. The black specks dotting the beach were not rocks. They let out a tiny gas that the visor could register but not identify. The beach moved up and down like a chest taking deep breaths.

"Hey Cooper, you know what those little black rock-looking

things are on the beach?" Jarvis waited for an answer as his drone whizzed by overhead. It was the last one they had left and that could spell trouble if Garay still had his. Jarvis ordered the drone to land on the deck. Eden came up from the armory in armor with her rifle still slung over her shoulder. Weddle closed his eBible and kissed his rifle before joining them.

Jarvis climbed up on the railing and stood on it with perfect balance. He repeated his question. "Cooper, are those things dangerous?"

"*Negative,*" Cooper's voice crackled through the intercom.

Jarvis jumped from the ship and hit sand. He felt a wave below the beach as if he had jumped onto a giant water bed. The little black things coughed up more steam, which smelled like a torn-open lower intestinal track. Jarvis turned his head away. The smell made his eyes water.

"*They're blow holes for something that is sleeping under the beach,*" Cooper informed him.

Jarvis laughed. "Well, it doesn't smell like it's breathing with them."

Jarvis took two steps and signaled the team to follow. Eden was next on the beach, followed by Burnett and Weddle. The black rocks spit up more gas and Jarvis started running to get past the beach and to reach relatively cleaner air. The empty tents sat back from the beach about three hundred yards. After he got past the foul-smelling air, he walked the rest of the way and the team caught up with him. About to enter a possibly hostile camp, they all fell into their training..

"*Relax no life signs,*" Cooper told them.

They knew not to believe Cooper's words. Garay knew a hundred different ways to cloak the signs of life. Jarvis signaled their shared neural net intercom. "*Stay out here and give me cover. No one in but me until I secure the camp.*"

Jarvis walked slowly between the first tents. The wind kicked up sand and blew heat and the tents flapped in the wind. It was an awful place and he couldn't think of a reason anyone wanted to set up camp here. Jarvis spun around and entered the first tent, his rifle ready.

The tent was empty of life but had four sleeping cots. The read-out on his visor scanned residual life signals, in an area devoid of life some traces could be detected for days.

He backed up and went to the next tent. This one was set up like a galley. Buckets of river water were set up with plates, and C-ration bags floated in it. There were still plates on the table with rotten food, and insects the size of footballs orbited over a C-ration attempt at a steak. It could have been there months or years; he had idea how long it took food to decompose on this world.

The flying insects beat their enormous wings wildly as they turned to him. Jarvis must have looked tastier than the steak. He stepped out and one of the giant bugs followed him, pushing the flap out of the way. He didn't want to shoot it and risk tipping his hand to anyone possibly hiding in the other tents. Jarvis grabbed the bug by the tail and pulled out a knife. It squeezed its goofy, slime-covered body and tried to slip out of his grip. He held on, stabbing it and slamming it to the ground. There was hard ground just under the sand. A second large bug came at him but this time he just grabbed something that felt like a neck. He squeezed and to his surprise, its head popped off.

"*Keep moving.*" Jarvis sent a signal as he ran to the next tent. He could feel Cooper watching from his net feed from the command center. Holding the flap open, he looked around. Two cots had been pushed together with a sheet over both; a couple slept here. Clothes and gear littered the tent floor. Jarvis saw a shirt half buried in the sand. He wasn't sure he wanted the others watching him, so he slid his visor up and disconnected his net-feed.

Cooper immediately sounded off over the internal intercom. "*I lost your picture.*"

Jarvis pushed the sand away and got a grip on the buried

shirt. He yanked on it. It looked like one of their uniforms, the ones they had worn since the Goddamn Killing Machines had been created. He felt something stiff in the upper pocket and had a moment of panic; it was the same pocket he had put the picture in the one that was missing when he woke up. He unzipped the pocket and a picture printed on paper landed face down.

He turned the photo over and felt a rush of heat on his skin, under his collar.

It was impossible. It was the missing photograph of Eden. Jarvis put the photo in his pocket and his breathing sped up.

"I can't find your net-feed and your numbers are spiking. Watch your heart rate." Cooper yelled.

Jarvis tried to think of when, how, or why Jamal Garay could have stolen that photo. It was impossible; the picture had been his secret for years. He felt caught and exposed. He straightened his back and took deep breaths. It was just a picture. He hadn't done anything wrong. They all suspected he and Eden had been in a relationship at one point.

He gripped the handle of his rifle and ran into the next tent, ignoring Cooper. He was afraid of what the man might find in Jarvis's thoughts. He wasn't sure what finding the photo meant. He couldn't let himself be distracted. He ran to the next tent. He smelled the rank odor before he pulled the flap open. Two of the giant bugs hovered and gnawed at a human corpse. Jarvis switched on his sound suppressor and fired two rounds.

The bugs exploded into a green puddle on the cot. Despite the silencer, Cooper saw read-outs of the shots register in the command center.

"What's happening Jarvis?" This time it was Eden.

"Hold the line! Don't move, you copy?" Jarvis yelled through his radio.

The radio buzzed. "Copy."

He walked closer to the body. It was a woman; had been a woman. It appeared she had struggled and her body twisted, her breasts mangled. It didn't appear to all be bites from the bugs, but he hoped he was wrong. The bugs had cleanly eaten away sections of her stomach. Parts of her arms and face were gone, like a puzzle missing pieces.

Jarvis stepped closer to the rotting body. There was enough left of her face for him to recognize her. Zana. It was impossible, he told himself, she was safe back on the ship, but he couldn't deny that it looked like her.

Jarvis turned away and walked out into the burning light of day. He turned the intercom back on. Before he could speak, he saw the light reflect off something buried in the sand. He walked towards it.

"Jarvis?" Eden called to him over the intercom.

Jarvis broke his silence. "Hey Burnett? What kind of pistol was that silver one Garay carried?"

"The silver Brazilian 9MM?" Burnett's voice boomed through Jarvis's head.

Jarvis pulled a silver Brazilian 9MM out of the sand. Old crusted blood covered the handle. The wind blew open the flap to the tent and he looked back at the mutilated body. The body that looked like Zana. His fingers stuck to the dried blood on the pistol and confusion and rage battled in his mind. Jarvis chucked the pistol into the dessert and ran back toward his team.

"Everybody back to the ship." He barked, motioning with his rifle for them to get moving.

Jarvis caught up to Eden and ran beside her. "What did you see?" she asked him.

He hesitated. "Not talking about it."

Burnett reached the ship first and waited by the ladder, ready to climb up. Jarvis stopped, wanting the big man to go first.

"That's a big camp for one target." Burnett shook his head. "I think I should get a look."

Jarvis looked back toward the camp. He didn't understand what happened there, not yet. He didn't understand what it all meant, but the last thing he needed was someone else seeing what he saw.

"I think you should get back on the fucking boat," Jarvis told him.

Burnett put one hand on the ladder but stared at Jarvis. "What the hell did you see out there, Jarvis?"

Jarvis hesitated and Burnett moved to step past him. Jarvis grabbed his rippling bicep and pushed him back against the ship, shaking his head. Jarvis was just as afraid that Burnett would see nothing, that he was crazy. No, he couldn't let Burnett pass. "I said get on the fucking ship; he moved on, we move on."

CHAPTER 24

TEN HOURS later they sped past the end of the desert. The trees began to thicken up again. Large herds of jurassus stood on two legs and yelled at the passing ship Jarvis noted that these northern ones had more hair than their counterparts in the south. They sounded like a thousand New York cabs honking during rush hour traffic. Jarvis watched them and wondered if they were saying hello or warning them about something up river.

"They should call this fucking river Styx. We all know what the end of line is." Weddle droned. They ignored his religious freak-out.

Jarvis had avoided the rest of the squad since getting back on the ship. He avoided looking at Zana when he put his armor away. He repeatedly saw flashes of the body. He was sure it was her, yet there she was at Cason's side, staring at the bag containing his body. He hadn't known her feelings for Cason ran so deep. Jarvis returned to deck to stare at the large planet taking up the majority of the sky. Weddle sat beside Burnett at the turret-gun, still talking to himself and holding his eBible as though he had flock.

"...End of the line is hell, we were doomed before we set foot on this rock. This river flows right into the gates of Hell and no god can forgive us for what we have done." Weddle continued his diatribe.

Jarvis watched him but knew telling him to shut his trap would only embolden him. Burnett would have done it for him, but he just blocked him out with music.

"Jamal Garay is a servant of the Evil One, when we cast him into the nether, the angels of God would tear our skin. Pull us into the burning pit; it is here in this garden of evil where we will pay for our sins."

Jarvis walked to the back of the ship so he could be alone. He leaned on the railing, staring into their wake. Every few seconds he saw a hicanus in the water; they were back and scratching at the hull.

Eden walked up beside him. Her bright hazel eyes looked stunning in the light of Beta and her hair gently stirred in the wind. He stared at her and thought of the picture hidden in his pocket.

He wondered if she would be angry if he showed her the picture.

Eden put her hand over his.

"What did you see in that camp?" Eden's voice was quiet.

The dragon-birds came swarming out of the jungle. Burnett let off a rocket and they went screaming away. It distracted them for a moment. Jarvis tried to walk away, but Eden blacked his path, forcing him back against the railing.

"Talk to me Nick," she demanded.

He smiled at her. "You know, that beach got me thinking."

She smiled back. "Oh yeah? The one that smelled like farts?"

"I mean, that was not a nice beach but I was thinking about how nice it is to relax. You know, on the beach." He wanted her to remember their time on Mars.

She knew something was up. "Like that time we got plastered in Argentina and..."

He shook his finger. "Nah, I was thinking about Mars."

"The lake beaches? It's not the same underground, I like real sun and sky at the beach." Eden laughed and Jarvis nodded.

"I mean, that is all you got on Mars beach-wise," Jarvis joked.

She looked at him, considering what he was up to. Jarvis looked away. Eden reached out and turned his face back to her.

"Hey, talk to me for real. You saw something out there." Her voice quieted again.

He felt a jolt where her hand touched his face. It calmed him and she sensed his relief. She rubbed his cheek and leaned in closer. Their eyes locked.

"I know you miss your boy," she whispered.

Any good feeling he felt drained away. Thinking about Sammy made him feel like a failure; he wasn't ready to accept that his boy was gone.

"I know it's hard, Nick, but we are family. A mean-as-hell, fucked-up-family, and we have to be here for each other." She pulled on his hips, leaned in, and pressed her lips softly to his. Nervously at first, they moved together before she nibbled at his bottom lip. Their lips separated and Jarvis leaned back against the railing. Eden leaned her body into his and tilted her eyes up to his. He noticed the picture of her folded in his pocket. Rage bubbled up into his chest. He pushed her away and left her standing there.

He was almost to the steps when a metal squealing stopped him short. Eden had punched the railing. Her recreated fist had bent the railing with a simple punch. She stared at her fist, shocked. Her hand should not have been that much stronger than a natural hand. Jarvis looked at his hands and squeezed. He thought back to that giant bug, he shouldn't have had the strength to pop its head straight off, but he did..

Eden turned to him. "What just happened?"

He shook his head; he opened his mouth to respond but was cut off by a scream. Zana. Eden was quicker and ran past him; Jarvis followed her down to the armory. Eden screamed and jumped back against the wall; Jarvis pulled out his gun but froze in the doorway. The body bag was sitting up; it looked like Cason was inside scratching to get out.

Cooper ran into the room. "Everyone out," he ordered.

Zana cried. Eden pulled her handgun out of her holster.

"What the fuck is happening," Jarvis screamed at Cooper.

"Get out!" Cooper yelled again.

Jarvis shook his head, and the scratching inside the body bag increased. Weddle appeared on the staircase, laughing like a maniac. Burnett walked down behind him and lifted his rifle when he saw the bag sitting up. The constant scratching of the hicanus under the ship added to the madness.

"This is going to get out of hand quickly, please just leave the room," Cooper pleaded.

Jarvis kept his gun high but reached over Cooper to grab the body bag's zipper. Cooper fought him and Jarvis was surprised at how strong the older man was. Eden took the opportunity to reach around both men and pulled the zipper down. Cason's head fell forward and his whole body shook. His eyes were empty but aside from the shaking, there were no other signs of life.

"Fuck!" Eden stepped back, holding her gun up.

"What the hell is happening?" Zana yelled, aiming her gun at Cooper's forehead as well.

Jarvis turned and slammed the door shut. Weddle and Burnett started banging on it. Jarvis grabbed Cason's head with both hands and looked into his face.

"He was fucking dead!" Zana screamed.

Eden shook her head disbelief. "One hard to kill mother-fucker - that Cason."

Jarvis continued to look into the man's eyes. "Cason?"

No reaction aside from a bit of drool. Jarvis turned back to Cooper, and then glanced at Zana. She understood his silent order and lowered her gun. Cooper let out a deep breath. Eden lowered her gun as well and opened the door to Burnett and Weddle.

"I don't remember telling you to relax," Jarvis let go of

Cason. "He was dead. I saw him with guts open and as pale as he could get. Why the fuck is he sitting up?"

Cooper shrugged. Jarvis grabbed him and dragged him out past the rest of the squad. Jarvis pushed him into the command center. Jammer jumped up when he saw Cooper hit the floor.

"Jammer get some fresh air," Jarvis ordered. Jammer looked around nervously.

"Now!"

Jammer ran from the room, slamming the door behind him. Cooper kept his eyes on the floor.

"What the fuck is really going on here? I'm not just talking about Cason. Back at that camp, I saw..." He wasn't sure he wanted to say it, he knew how it sounded.

Cooper smiled and laughed a devilish chuckle. "You saw what?"

Jarvis straightened his arm, raising his pistol to the man's skull.

"Put it down," whispered Cooper.

Jarvis pulled the hammer back. *Just pull the trigger and get the fuck out of here.* Suddenly the lights went out in the command center and started flashing red. The intercom went off inside Jarvis' neural net.

"Self destruct sequence initiated."

Cooper pushed the gun away. Outside the room the rest of the squad reacted, someone started banging on the door. Jarvis and Cooper stared at each other for a long moment. Jarvis felt sweat forming like a rook on his first fight.

"You forgot one little detail." Cooper straightened his shirt. "I'm in fucking charge!"

Jarvis put the gun back in his holster. "Call it off."

"I don't know why Cason is alive, or even if that's the right word." Cooper looked away from him.

Jarvis knew he was lying.

Cooper pointed at the door. "No more questions, from you OR them!"

Cooper walked over and opened the door. Eden waited on the other side. She was sweating, breathing hard.

"Now I'm going to take a look at Cason." Cooper walked out leaving Eden and Jarvis alone. Eden wanted something from him, but Jarvis was too angry to think straight.

CHAPTER 25

THE SHIP CONTINUED to head up river, but they didn't pay much attention to what was coming towards them. Everyone was focused on what was happening in the armory, even if they had no idea what that was. They spent a lot of time looking at the door. Jarvis ordered them on to the deck and back into the heat.

Cooper had locked himself away with Cason and had been in there for almost twenty minutes. They heard two random screams from Cason, but mostly silence. Jarvis sat at the top of the stairs, blocking the others from coming off the deck. The squad stood behind him feeling useless. Weddle continued with his religious babble while Zana and Burnett hovered over Jarvis, ready to storm down the steps and open fire.

Jarvis put his hand up to stop them.

"This is insane, we need to go down there and put Cason out of his misery," Burnett argued.

Zana looked up at Burnett. "No, it's Cooper. We need to kill that lying piece of shit."

Jarvis kept his eyes focused on the basement steps.

"Can't do it. If Cooper's heart stops, or his brain stops working, then boom," said Jarvis. His eyes never moved.

Eden leaned over Jarvis's shoulder. "We need to know what is going on in there."

Jarvis stood up and walked over to a vent that was belching out hot air from inside the ship. He used his knife to unscrew the bolt holding it on. Without a word, his drone took flight and appeared over his shoulder. It went into silent mode and slowed its speed as it ducked into the now-open air duct.

Jarvis turned back to the squad and put his finger over his mouth. He didn't share the images with anyone as the drone used night-shot telemetry from inside the duct.

"Bullshit Jarvis, give us the goddamn telemetry," Burnett said.

Jarvis turned and got right up in Burnett's face. He shook his head slowly. "Forget it."

The drone moved through the tunnel until it came up against the grates to the armory. The camera zoomed as it focused on Cooper working on Cason.

Cason was face down, tied to the table and the back of his head and skull were cracked open like a door. Blood and brains littered the table, next to a saw that Cooper used to cut his way in. Jarvis switched on the microphone as the image enlarged. Cason moved slightly and his fingers twitched. Not one drop of blood flowed from his head.

Back on the deck, Jarvis stood watching the footage, stunned silent.

"What do you see?" asked Eden.

Everyone stared at him, waiting for an answer.

Jarvis ignored Eden and focused on the images beamed back from the drone. He zoomed the lens closer. He couldn't believe his eyes: there was no brain. Only wires, chips, and a wetware interface globe the size of a golf ball. He didn't have time to react to what he saw when Burnett screamed out in pain.

He turned see a group of dragon-birds biting Burnett's shoulders. They were larger now, but it took all four biting and pulling at him to lift Burnett off his feet. He shot wildly as he was dropped and his back hit the deck. The wild shots almost hit Weddle, and a group of dragon-birds narrowly missed him as he dove out of the way.

Realization ran through them all at the same time: *they forgot about the gas!*

Up above them sky filled with screaming dragon-birds. Back down in the command center, Jammer turned the ship to get away from them but only crashed into a sand bank. Zana lifted her rifle to fire but as the ship hit the sand, she shot wild. Bullets shot across the deck and tore up Burnett.

Weddle ran to the railing and jumped off the side of the ship. Jarvis pulled both his pistols out of their holsters and dropped onto the deck, rolling as he fired at the dragon-birds. He turned his head and saw Weddle run into the jungle. Eden crawled across the deck, trying to get to Burnett's rifle while the dragon-birds bit and scratched at her back. Jarvis looked like he was aiming at her and she flinched as he fired inches over her head. The dragon-birds blew apart in an oozy mess over her back. With her eyes closed, Eden reached out and pulled at Burnett's rifle. His dying hands stiffened around it.

Jarvis lay on his back and pointed both handguns straight up and fired. The pistols could fire for 2,000 rounds before the self-replicating ammo was spent. Each dragon-bird he blew apart rained blood and guts down on him.

Eden continued to pull at Burnett's rifle; she almost had it when it snapped back toward him. He suddenly sat up and pointed the rifle, even though his body was a bloody mess. Eden ducked and covered her head. Burnett launched the rocket. The gas exploded and rained down on them. The dragon-birds scurried away toward the jungle, following Weddle.

Jarvis rolled over and shook the dragon-bird's guts off his uniform. He felt the dust from the rocket launcher land on him and knew would repel the dragon-birds for at least an hour. Zana was already up on the railing, going after Weddle.

"Zana! Stop!" Jarvis yelled at her.

She turned back. "We can't just leave him out there alone."

Eden propped Burnett up; he heaved, and breathed heavy.

Strickland ran to the railing and tried to grab Zana. "Fuck that crazy asshole, he ran out there; his problem."

Zana eluded him and jumped on to the rocky shore. Jarvis holstered his pistols and grabbed Strickland's rifle.

"Get a med-kit and patch Burnett up," he ordered.

Strickland shook his head. "Are you crazy? He just took a dozen bullets."

Burnett grunted and tried to get up. "I ain't gonna make it."

The dragon-birds screamed like banshees deep in the jungle. Jarvis pushed Strickland toward Burnett. "Try! We need everybody if we're going to stop Garay."

Jarvis could not let Zana and Weddle go either. He jumped over the railing and landed on the rocky shoreline. As he ran he realized the ground was not soft like an Earth jungle. Instead, it was similar to concrete but not quite as hard. The trees swayed away from his path as he entered the woods. The dragon-birds circled as close they could get, screaming a rhythmic ear-drum-rattling falsetto when they smelled the gas on his skin. They wanted to eat him but were repelled by the gas, so they swirled just above his head. In the distance, he heard automatic rounds firing. Weddle was lighting up the jungle.

Moss-covered vines came alive and moved across the jungle floor as they reached and snapped for him. More gunfire, closer now.

"Zana!" Jarvis caught up to her and she fired at the ground around her feet. The vine-creatures snapped at her. Jarvis came up behind her and pushed her in the direction of Weddle's gunfire.

"Where the fuck is he going?" Zana screamed as she kept firing at their feet.

"No clue!" Jarvis shouted back.

The jungle floor crawled around them. The trees shook and fell toward each other as the ground moved like a wave. Jarvis grabbed Zana and she leaned against a boulder; it rolled and they both fell. Jarvis fired to his right and the vines held back. He heard Zana scream as a vine twisted around her leg. Her hand gripped his arm like a vice.

A vine slipped up her back and around her neck. She tried to scream as her face turned purple. Jarvis jumped on top of her like a lover. One eye was closed and the other tried to stay open as Zana fought to breathe. Jarvis felt woozy in the heat, even after days of it. He had seen this woman dead before. Jarvis shook his head and questioned his sanity.

Zana struggled to bring air into her lungs. Jarvis threw her rifle to the ground. He pulled his knife under the vine to cut it. It was solid as stone. Jarvis grunted as he pushed the knife slowly through. He barely cut it.

He heard a snap but it wasn't the vine. Her neck broke twice. The sound he heard was her neck breaking in two places. Her head twisted sideways at an impossible angle. Her eyes remained open, and her hands continued to struggle for a few seconds. Jarvis picked up her rifle and stared at Zana as her eyes froze open.

Gunfire peppered the air in the distance; it was Weddle. Jarvis jumped up, hating to leave Zana but knew there was nothing he could do. He felt the vines grabbing at his feet but managed to stay ahead of them. He got closer to the gunfire. His internal neural net said that Weddle was less than a hundred feet away. Weddle's net was not accepting orders, but he could detect his life signs.

Jarvis reached a point where the vines stopped grabbing at him. Weddle stood in one spot firing down.

"Weddle!" Jarvis yelled at him.

Weddle kept firing. As Jarvis got closer he saw a trail of blood leading from another path in the jungle. Weddle had been torn to shreds, his uniform and skin hanging off his frame like melting cheese shreds. Missing an ear and holding his rifle with the one arm he had remaining, Weddle kept firing into a pit before him.

Jarvis stopped ten feet from Weddle. A group of dragon-birds fought on the ground over morsels of Weddle's missing arm. They screamed a warning to Jarvis but he stepped up to the arm and they scurried away from his smell. He looked down at the mess that was Weddle's arm. There was no bone. Broken pieces of metal shaped like an arm bone glinted in the sunlight. Jarvis called out to Weddle again as the head of a giant dragon-bird lifted out of the pit in front of him. The dragon-bird opened its large mouth and screamed. The creature's hot breath rolled over them and made Jarvis feel weak-kneed.

Weddle lifted his rifle to fire at it, its' large mouth snapping down on him. The mouth latched on to the top of his head and pulled back, pulling his body to its knees. The top half of his head was now gone. Weddle's body fell backwards with a thump. Jarvis expected half his brain and a pool of blood to escape. There was blood, but instead of brain, pieces of torn wetware and tiny fingernail-sized computer chips flowed out with the crimson river. Jarvis stepped closer and saw the giant dragon-bird laying on its back in the pit, ejecting eggs. One of the eggs hatched and Jarvis watched a thousand tiny screaming dragon-birds. Weddle had destroyed several eggs, which were spitting out thousands of half-formed, screaming dragon-bird hatchlings.

Jarvis stepped back and prayed that the gas Cooper created scared off adult dragon-birds as well as the hatchlings. The Queen dragon-bird lifted her head toward him and Jarvis ran backwards, firing a short burst of bullets. The Queen screamed but kept her distance.

The jungle felt hotter as he ran. The image of the path waved in front of him. He stopped to catch his breath and consider everything he saw. Jarvis put his hands on his knees and stared at the ground. Tiny worm-looking vines crawled in every direction.

Over his labored breath, he heard the dragon-birds getting closer, their numbers growing by the second. Jarvis straightened and saw the ship at the far end of the trail. He took a deep breath and ran back to the ship, a horrible question playing repeatedly in his head: *Who was really human among them?*

CHAPTER 26

CASON, *Weddle, Zana...they weren't human. They couldn't be.*

It seemed impossible. Technology now was able to clone a human but the clone might not grow up to be similar, and they built synthetic humans, but those acted just like computers in subtle ways. Human programming and subtle human behaviors were different. In the last hundred years, AI computers and androids had made many advancements, but the variations in human behavior were such that it was impossible to make a passable human.

He had known those members of his team for decades, fought beside them, and been as close to hell and back as a person could come. He trained them from pups to killers and they were feared on multiple planets. He knew what made them laugh, cry, or ready to pop off. He didn't notice anything different, besides Weddle finding God, but that wasn't so strange; he has always been unhinged a bit.

It was impossible. Or was it?

According to Cooper, hundreds of years had slipped past them. Who knew what kind of technology existed out here? Jarvis stopped a few feet from the ship, the river raging past quicker than it seemed when he was on the ship. He could barely see the other side of the river it was so wide. They had already traveled a distance longer than any river that existed on Earth.

He felt stupid for getting himself into this mess.

Jarvis heard a gunshot as he climbed back on to the ship. He found Eden holding a bleeding Burnett up against a wall. Cooper wiped blood off his own lip; he had a red bump on the side of his head that was already starting to bruise. Burnett was not doing well if Eden controlled him so easy. Jarvis didn't have the energy to even ask what happened.

He stared at Cooper, who knew that Jarvis was angry. Cooper looked Jarvis up and down; two animals sizing each other up for an attack.

"Where is Zana?" Cooper asked. "Weddle?"

When Jarvis didn't answer, Eden let out a sigh. Burnett cursed under his breath.

"Jammer – Let's get the fuck out of here." Jarvis said.

Eden let go of Burnett who slumped down to the floor. Eden turned Jarvis around.

"Wait, are you sure? Strickland and I can do a search," she told him.

Strickland turned around from his seat at the turret-gun. "What? Fuck that! I'm not getting off this boat," he yelled.

"Real brave, Strickland," Eden shot him a dirty look. "How did you get on this squad missing your balls?"

Eden grinned but Strickland didn't look amused. Jarvis knew Strickland's sense of humor was gone and all he wanted was to get off this rock. The engine rumbled to life while Cooper and Jarvis just stared at each other. The ship pulled off down the river. The dragon-birds followed and screamed at a safe distance above them. Eden's eyes ping-ponged between them, knowing an unspoken anger was coming to a boil.

"Galley now!" Jarvis gave the command, and everyone on the deck stopped.

Cooper cleared his throat. "I was just going to suggest we have a private talk."

Jarvis grabbed Cooper by his uniform shoulder but Cooper

pulled away as they went down the stairs. Heading into the room, Cooper sat down at one of the tables and propped his feet up; a blatant attempt to not look intimidated. Jarvis slammed the door. He wanted answers.

Hundreds of years had passed, they had traveled four light years, been attacked and lost lives. Through it all Cooper had control. Jarvis felt his anger boiling over. He knew exactly what was happening. Jarvis jumped forward and threw Cooper up against the wall. Cooper grunted.

"Let go of me or I will blow this..." Cooper's words were choked off as Jarvis punched him in the stomach. Cooper keeled to his knees.

"Do it, you piece of shit!" Jarvis yelled at him.

Cooper stared up, wide-eyed. Jarvis lifted him by the collar and dragged him so their faces were inches apart.

"My son is dead, I'm roasting ten thousand kilometers up the flowing asshole of the universe, and you think I'm afraid of you blowing us to hell. Do it! End this bullshit."

Cooper stared, confused. For the first time he had nothing to say.

Jarvis shook him again. "Why us? Of all the killers in this fucking galaxy?"

Jarvis saw something click in the man's eyes. Cooper smirked. "Pull your head out of your ass for a minute and you'd see you DO have something to live for."

Jarvis pulled Cooper even closer so that the old man could smell his breath. Cooper grimaced and turned his face. Jarvis tightened his grip. "I saw you with Cason, with his head open on the table."

That got Cooper's attention, but it was subtle; he was trying to hide his reaction.

"And Weddle? I don't know what died out there in that

jungle, but that wasn't Weddle. It was some kind of android. I'm not sure about Zana, but I've seen her dead now...twice."

Cooper laughed, a fake sound. "Pull yourself together Jarvis. This jungle is fucking with you."

"Maybe. I thought I was crazy before. Now I've got telemetry from the drone of you and Cason."

Cooper rolled his eyes. "You start showing that around and you doom this mission."

"What mission?" Jarvis barked.

Cooper fought to free himself. Jarvis finally let go.

Cooper straightened his uniform and pointed a finger at Jarvis. "You made a monster. You have no idea how out of control that monster is, but we're here to kill it. You see this through, and you'll learn everything. But I'll warn you now, you might not be so happy you pressed the issue."

CHAPTER 27

Jarvis walked up on deck. The ship headed down river fast and his drone was back in the air following a new search pattern. The dragon-birds still circled and the hicanus matched the ship's speed, continuing to scratch away at the bottom. The jungle changed; trees at this part were the width of buildings and looked similar to the old northern forests on Earth, forests long gone. The sound, heat, and stink of the jungle didn't fade; just hung over the ship like a pregnant storm cloud.

Most of the crew who remained waited on deck and they stared at Jarvis as he approached. They wanted answers. Jarvis looked at Eden first, then Strickland. Burnett bled on the deck, wincing in pain. Jammer was down in the command center.

What were they? Androids? Cyborgs? Could he trust them? If they were androids, could Cooper have programmed them? Would they listen to his commands? Jarvis looked from face to face as these questions raced through his mind.

Eden joined him. The heat was so intense he saw wavy heat lines distorting Strickland, who remained at the turret-gun. Jarvis leaned on the deck, sweating. Eden took his arm and moved gently pulled him toward the steps.

"When was the last time you had water?" she asked.

Jarvis looked at her, confused. He didn't know how to respond.

"We're all sweating buckets, you need to hydrate," she insisted.

His vision blurred. He glanced at Burnett, who looked ready to die.

"Somebody get him in the AC," said Jarvis.

Strickland didn't even turn around. "I'm not leaving this gun."

Jarvis tried arguing but Eden pushed him harder toward the stairs. It was a blur; she led him to the galley but the next thing he knew he was sitting, a cold glass of water in his hands. He stared at it. The air conditioning made his skin pucker, goose-fleshing in the cold. He was too exhausted to rub his arms and warm them. He continued to stare at the water in the glass.

"Drink it." Eden's voice was hard.

Jarvis looked up; she looked human. He looked at her skin and noticed that her skin didn't change in the cold air. She crossed her arms, and he felt guilty. He gulped his water and wondered if artificial humans or copies in this advanced time were now fully functional. His eyes sank to her rounded hips. She pulled up a chair and sat next to him.

"Hey, eyes up here." Eden motioned two fingers at her own eyes, smiling.

He looked into them. The deep green was as mesmerizing as he remembered. Their eyes locked, and she smiled wider, tipping her head slightly. He liked how her hair hung when she did that. It seemed like Eden, the real Eden. She always smiled at him, even in the worst cluster-fucks. In the back of his mind, he knew that was because she loved him, deeply. He never wanted to admit it, but he loved her back and didn't feel he could act on it.

A thousand variables made up the nuance of a human. He loved the details of Amanda Eden. It was hard for him to believe that an AI could fool him.

She put her hand on his face. He felt a sheen of sweat on her palm.

Could a geek in a lab design a being with that level of detail? Jarvis wondered.

"What did Cooper tell you?" Eden asked.

He wanted to tell her. But didn't know what was real, who was real. What if Cooper had programmed her to ask? What if he was using her? He could tip his hand to Cooper; if he told him too much and he would use it against him. He shouldn't have said anything. Jarvis put his hand over hers on his cheek.

"We need to complete the mission," he told her.

Her face registered disappointment. Jarvis felt his gut churn; he didn't want to let her down. She looked around and lowered her voice to a whisper. "We have to kill him."

Jarvis leaned back. *This could be a test.* "Kill who?"

Eden leaned in again. "You know who."

Jarvis slid his chair back and stood up; he filled his cup with water. "No, we have to complete the mission."

Eden looked stunned. "What? Why? He lied to you, to us."

Eden didn't normally question him like this; she had always trusted his judgment. He stared at her, looking for a flaw, something that wasn't right. He found nothing; it was the same face he saw every night when he closed his eyes. She stepped closer and Jarvis thrilled by her proximity. *Part of the test?*

"He lied Nick. He promised you would see your son again," Eden sighed.

Jarvis turned away. A tight rubber band inside his chest was pulling to the breaking point. He silently counted to ten; anything to keep his mind off his boy, that other life. "Just stop," he whispered.

"Sammy is dead." Eden's voice hardened.

Something snapped inside when he heard his son's name. He spun and made the fist without thinking. He hesitated and Eden responded quickly. She punched, knocking him sideways and dumping the glass of water all over them. Jarvis touched his lip and looked at blood on his finger. Split lip, right down the middle. He turned but she was already swinging again, knocking him down. The glass shattered on the floor.

Eden fell on top of him; she sat on his chest, her fist balled and ready to punch again. He put his hands on her bare legs, just below her shorts. She hit him again; he didn't fight as her fist pounded his face.

Tears welled up and she screamed. "You fucking bastard. I wanted you. YOU! He could have been ours."

She took another swing and he blocked it, grabbing her wrist. She fought to free herself and slipped down, their faces inches apart. She breathed heavy, and Jarvis closed his eyes. He felt her breasts against his uniform with each fervent breath. She pressed her lips against his, a violent attack until it lessened. She pressed him against the floor and slipped her hands under his shirt.

Jarvis ripped at her shirt and yanked it off. They rolled awkwardly on the floor, pulling each other's clothes free. Eden finally jerked her knife from its sheath and just cut away his belt. Hooking her fingers around his pants and the band on his boxer's, she slid them off with one motion. Jarvis caressed every inch of her smooth back before stripping her shorts to her ankles. Their gun holsters thumped into each other on the floor.

He took a deep breath and she arched slid on top of him; he slowly shifted and entered her. She exhaled as pent up desire released. Eden continued to grind even as she collapsed on him, she was shaking, losing track of time, her energy almost spent. He kissed her neck, she kissed his ear.

"I always wanted you," he whispered.

He rolled over gently so she could rest on the floor. He felt himself ready to climax. He slowed down and her legs twisted behind his back. Jarvis kissed her neck, wanting to taste every inch of her. He lowered his lips to her right nipple. Sucking on the hard skin, his cut lip ached. He felt a tiny hair on his lip. It was soft and tiny just below the nipple.

It stopped him. It was natural and normal. There was something very human about the imperfection. He swelled with passion.

He lifted his head. She tugged on his hips, trying to pull him back toward her. Despite the air conditioning their skin burned hot and they were both dripping sweat. Here it was, a moment he fantasized about for years. She was real: this was his Eden. He smiled at her, knowing that despite every storm, they made it to this moment. Eden's legs tightened behind his back and her body was warm around him. She squeezed like a heart pumping for the final time and he pushed deeper, ready to scream.

He loved her deeply and forever.

CHAPTER 28

DRIFTING in that sweet spot between deep sleep and full awareness, Jarvis kept his eyes closed and listened to Eden's breath. He lay across her, his face resting on her flat belly. He listened to her stomach, comforted to hear the natural gurgles and rumbles of digestion. It was the beautiful sound of human function. He fell in and out of sleep, more relaxed than he had been in months of relative time.

"I think I know how to disable Cooper's link to the self-destruct." Eden whispered and woke Jarvis up. She must have been worried that Cooper was listening. He didn't want to ask her for details.

He sat up slightly. "Why haven't you done it?"

"It will only last a minute at the most. We'll have to act before he realizes it's happening." Eden propped her head up on one hand and looked down at him.

He opened his mouth to respond when everything suddenly gotten quiet.

The hicanus' scratching had stopped. Jarvis stared at the broken glass and the pile of clothes on the floor. Their incessant clawing hadn't stopped for days, and had actually increased since they'd gotten a taste of Cason's blood. Those beasts had followed them and scratched endlessly at the bottom of the hull since they had landed in the river. It was like an unending choir of fingernails on chalkboards, and the sudden, absolute silence now that they had stopped shocked him.

Jarvis sat up first, and Eden gasped when they saw Cooper in the doorway with his arms crossed. He laughed.

"I came to tell you something's happening, but it looks like you know that." Cooper arched one brow.

Eden scooted behind Jarvis but Jarvis made no attempt to hide his nakedness.

"Get out of here," he told Cooper.

Cooper mock saluted and turned his back on them. "You might want to get dressed and get out here."

He walked out of the room. Jarvis turned to Eden and she grinned. He kissed her, their lips touching softly. He couldn't bring himself to pull away.

"We better go," she whispered.

Jarvis sifted through the pile and tossed her shorts, underwear, and uniform top over to her. He put his pants on. It had been days since they had this kind of silence and calm. He grabbed a piece of paper and started drawing on it. She watched as he drew and then as he folded up the paper.

Jarvis didn't want to leave this room; that meant going back to reality. He was nervous about asking her, but he had to. "What does this mean?" He gestured to the floor, indicating what had just occurred between them.

She tilted her head; his knees got weak every time she smiled that way. Her bottom lip got fat like a child pouting.

She shrugged. "I don't know." She reached up and grabbed his arm. "Wait – I think it means we need to live through this."

That stopped him. He angrily recalled what Cooper said about having something to live for. The old man must have seen what Jarvis had refused to allow into his head. He didn't have time to think about it now. The intercom signaled his neural net.

Everybody come to the command center now! Cooper's voice boomed through.

Eden turned to run out of the room but Jarvis grabbed her and spun her into a kiss. His hand slid the paper into her back pocket. Their lips parted just enough for his whisper.

"Don't look at this unless I tell you. Promise?"

She kissed him back passionately to signal her agreement. She took off, giving him a few seconds to pull himself together.

Jarvis straightened his uniform as he followed her to the command center. Burnett was now loaded with painkillers; Strickland flipped one of his knives nervously. Jammer and Cooper worked the controls. Strickland shook his head in disbelief at Eden and Jarvis.

"About goddamn time," Strickland muttered.

Jarvis pointed at one of the screens. "What happened to the hicanus?"

Jammer turned in his chair. "They freaked out. About a half click back there was some energy pulse. It traveled up the river and they took off on shore to the east. I stopped the ship."

Cooper forwarded drone telemetry to everyone. The jurassus had run away from the river as well.

"The primates, the birds; everything is taking off in a frenzy. When the pulse vibrated through, our drone saw the same reaction further north. Even the little dragon-birds have scattered."

They glanced back and forth at each other for a long silent moment. Strickland broke the silence. "OK, who farted?"

Burnett kicked him. Tense laughter trickled through the room.

Cooper shrugged. "It's not the dumbest question. Who or what is scaring these things off?"

"Was the pulse biological in nature?" asked Eden.

Cooper clasped his hands in his lap. "It appears to be some kind of technology."

Jammer interjected, "We don't know for sure because it's different."

Jarvis pointed at Strickland, then Eden. "Strickland, get back on the big gun. Eden, get a rifle and get up top. Jammer, I need you to fight on deck."

Jammer's jaw almost dropped off. Jarvis tugged on his uniform; he knew it wasn't right to ask Jammer to fight, but they were down a few men already. Burnett couldn't fight in his condition, but he could steer the ship. Cooper nodded in silent agreement.

A few hours had passed since Jarvis had been out in the heat and burning light, the heat was a slap in the face; nothing about it felt good. Jarvis cursed it inwardly as sweat began dripping down his body. Eden and Jammer followed him on the deck. Strickland ran straight to the turret-gun.

It was the first time in a long time, probably several Earth days, which the sky above them had been clear. It had been hard to see the large gas giant spinning above them because the sky had been filled with dragon-birds. Now they had a clear view. Jarvis really hated this moon.

"Jarvis!" Eden yelled.

Jarvis ran to the back of the ship. Jammer cursed under his breath and loaded the first round into the chamber of his rifle. Downriver, hundreds of little streaks came towards them just under the water line, like torpedoes.

"Burnett! Get us the fuck out of here," Jarvis yelled back through his neural net.

The engine rumbled to life as the torpedoes closed in. Eden and Jammer opened fire into the water. The first round of torpedoes surged through the water and slammed into the ship. The ship tipped to one side and they had to stop firing to grab on to the railing. There was no explosion. Jarvis looked up just as a second round of torpedoes came toward them. This set rose out of the water flew toward the deck. Eden and Jarvis let go of the railings and fell back, firing both pistols.

Once the torpedoes were in the air, they looked like inkblots spread over a ball. When the bullets hit them, they exploded splashing down into the clear river water. It was like shooting water balloons. One of the balls ejected an octopus-like creature that landed and slid on the deck. More tentacled creatures launched out of the river like water from a fire hose, raining down on the deck and all its occupants. Strickland turned around and fired shot after shot at the inkblots over their heads. Jarvis was certain this was the end, and for Jammer it was.

CHAPTER 29

JARVIS DIDN'T HEAR it over the sound of the guns. There was thump as Jammer fell face-first into the deck. Projectile after projectile came at them but exploded into water when they shot them each ejecting a creature at the same time. They were soaked but unharmed. Several fist-sized octopus-like beasts squirmed on the deck and slowly died. Jammer convulsed; one of the octopus creatures had attached itself to the back of his head. Eden was pulling at its slime-covered body but it held tight.

Jarvis stopped firing as the inkblot projectiles slowed down to float just over the deck; they perfectly matched the speed of the ship, hovering around them. They were like floating eyes, watching him. Eden strained but couldn't pull the creature off Jammer. With each of her hard tugs, the creature seemed to hold on tighter.

Jarvis watched the inkblots float. Eden gave up on Jammer, picked her rifle up, and turned around. She pointed her gun, but didn't fire. Jarvis still had both pistols in his hand, but also held his fire. Strickland had stopped firing the big gun.

Larger inkblots jumped out of the water and floated toward Strickland and he spun and pointed the large gun back at them, inches over the deck.

"No, wait, don't fire!" Jarvis waved his arms.

It was too late; a burst of gunfire tore through the huge inkblots, splashing gallons of water on the deck. Larger octopi-creatures burst from the inkblots and fell to the deck. One landed on eight limbs and scooted across the deck toward Strickland with amazing speed. He pointed the gun at it. Eden and Jarvis both screamed at him, waving their hands.

"NO!" They yelled in unison. They could both see what Strickland was too energized to realize. He was aiming right at the ship's deck.

It was too late. Strickland fired, tearing up the deck. The octopi-creature was the size of a throne and it scaled the gun at him. Bullets exploded in a straight line again, cutting through the floor and causing Eden to jump out of the way.

"What the fuck?" Eden screamed at Strickland.

"*Cease fire!*" First Burnett and then Cooper screamed over the intercom. They probably had to dodge at least one of the bullets that had ripped through the command center.

Strickland screamed. One of the creature's eight limbs jabbed at his chest, knocking a football-sized hole in it. Strickland's face froze as one tentacle pulled out his beating heart, leaving his chest a blood-soaked mess. The octopi-creature turned around. Jarvis lifted one pistol and fired a single shot. The top half of the creature burst into a multi-colored liquid and oozed off the front of the ship. The inkblots circled them, tightening their ranks.

"It ripped his fucking heart out!" Jarvis yelled.

They continued to circle slowly and silently. Jarvis heard water splashing under the ship and Eden's heavy breath, but aside from that it was silent. He saw inside the inkblots now that they were closer; the small octopi-creatures floated inside. These were smaller versions of the same things that had stared at them when they first landed. The ball floating in front of his face turned until the creatures faced him. Jarvis assumed what he was looking at was a face; he could see something blinking like an eye near the top of its body.

"What the fuck is it?" Eden asked. She had fallen to the deck and remained there.

"The natives, I think." Jarvis holstered his pistols and poked the inkblot with a finger. It felt like a slimy bubble, or a greasy balloon.

"Some kind of octopus." Jarvis looked around at hundreds of these floating balls of water. They continued speeding along with them. "Cooper, you seeing this?"

The intercom crackled across his neural net. *"Jarvis, we're blind down here, we can't see or hear much of anything."*

"We have casualties, we're surrounded by some kind of flying balloon. They're softball-sized and filled with..." Jarvis hesitated for a moment, looking for the right way to describe these things.

Cooper finished for him,"Water and some eight-limbed things? They grow bigger when they come out of the shell?" Jarvis sighed. He knew who or what these things were.

"I think they want to talk," said Jarvis.

"Or have a staring contest," quipped Eden. She stood and stepped closer to one of the floating blobs.

Jammer suddenly flipped over twice. He looked like a fish out of water flapping and trying to breathe. Suddenly he sat up, his eyes wide. His mouth opened and shut several times before he spoke. The octopi-creature attached to him humped the back of his head as he spoke.

"Uh tock, rock na pa doh, ahhh."

Jammer shook his head and repeated the nonsense. Eden lifted her rifle; Jarvis pointed his pistol. The flying blobs spun around, distracting them while Jammer struggled to move, like a fawn taking baby steps.

"Uh craaa to juk na."

Eden now saw that the octopi-creature caused the back of Jammer's head to bleed each time he spoke.

"Get off him!" Eden raised the rifle and the blobs floated to create a barrier between her rifle and Jammer's head. Jammer's body spoke again.

"Welcome, uh craa Juka Greetings Pa Doh, ahhh. Hola."

Jarvis pushed Eden's rifle down, and the blobs lifted up revealing Jammer's face, now frozen in a shit-eating grin.

"We choose uh craa doh, this partially biological being, uh doh ra ta..."

Jammer's head shook for a moment as if he was having seizure. Then calm came over him and the creature stopped humping the back of his head. Octopi-Jammer spoke in a smooth, radio-friendly voice.

"...as a means to communicate. Forgive us as we are still assimilating your language. We speak through a system of gestures and releases of oil."

Eden and Jarvis shared a quick glance. Octopi-Jammer stepped closer. His skin desiccated, his body was now a dried out hull. The creature was draining him of liquid to stay alive.

"I represent a culture known as the Hung-niya. We live under the great ocean in vast ..." it paused searching for a word. "...Cities."

It sucked the liquid out of Jammer's body like a straw in the back of his head. The Hung-niya lived under water and these floating inkblots were like spaceships. Coming out of their ocean was pretty much the same idea for them as hopping a spaceship and traveling across the universe was for Jarvis and his team. Cooper tried to get the intercom to work, but it just crackled, no voice coming through.

Octopi-Jammer continued, his voice getting raspier with each word. "You must leave this world; it is home to my people, who do not wish to share."

Jarvis nodded and put his hands up. "We don't want to be here. We have one thing to do and--"

"You want this over-world to be a home to your kind," Octopi-Jammer accused him.

"No, not really. Actually, I really fucking hate this planet," Jarvis shook his head.

A new inkblot spun out of the circle and to the front of Octopi-Jammer's head. The Octopi -creature inside moved its tentacles wildly. Octopi –Jammer watched it for a moment, and then turned Jammer's head back to Jarvis.

"My mate assures me that they have warned you before," it said.

"Maybe my people but not us." Jarvis looked around at Eden, who shrugged.

"My mate assures me it was you."

"Well, you all look alike to me."

Jammer's skin had almost turned to leather, his dried-out skin hanging off his skeleton.

"You invaders must leave," Octopi-Jammer's voice cracked as the body it controlled dried out and began to fall apart.

Jarvis looked at Eden again. He wasn't sure how long they had left to talk to the creature. "We are only here to kill one of our fellow invaders; once we do that we'll leave. Please, you have my word."

A section of Jammer's skin fell off his frame and his uniform fell open. His organs had turned to dust and blew out of his rib cage. The body shook and the voice became raspier as the vocal chords started to shrivel up.

"We shall lead you to the invader."

The vocal cords burst into dust, the octopi-creature detached from Jammer's head and leaped into the air. It landed against one of the inkblots, sinking into it. The intercom snapped back on.

"Jarvis!"

"Yeah, we're here." He looked at Strickland and then what was left of Jammer's body. It looked as if it had been rotting in the sun for months. "Jammer and Strickland are dead."

One of the large inkblots flashed various colors and headed to the front of the ship, stopping to hang over the turret-gun.

"Cooper, you see that giant flashy ball thing?" Jarvis asked.

"Yeah?"

"Follow it where ever it goes."

The rest of the inkblots now blocked out the sky. They hung over their ship as they navigated behind the large floating ball.

They circled back down the river. Jarvis wasn't surprised they had over shot their target.

Eden walked toward Jammer's body. "What did he mean by 'partially biological being?'"

Jarvis looked at Eden and his eyes widened. "Get back!" He pushed her toward the stairs. "Get below deck now."

Eden looked at him, surprised by his outburst. Anger and then sadness flickered over her face. Jarvis saw that she was considering not listening to him.

"Amanda, I need you to go below deck. Plan C."

She was surprised to hear her first name, more surprised to hear the order, that was part of the team's secret language. "Plan C?" Recognition lit up her face and she turned and ran below, slamming the door. After he was sure the door shut safely behind her, Jarvis turned off the visual part of his feed.

"Jarvis, I lost visual." Burnett told him what he already knew.

"Just a minute," he responded.

Jarvis leaned down and looked at Jammer's body moving the uniform aside with the end of one pistol barrel. The bones and rib cage dripped blood but they were not made of bone. A white powder blew off the bones into the wind. The bones were pure steel. The skin on Jammer's head flaked away. Using the gun barrel, he nudged the bottom of the jaw up and looked past the teeth. They too were flaking away to reveal steel.

You can replace almost everything, but the human brain. If he had been human there would be a dried up brain looking like a raisin.

He swung the butt of the gun down on the skull. It crackled easily, like an eggshell, but nothing drained out. All that remained in the skull was a wetware assembly connected to nano-tubes.

CHAPTER 30

"NICK?"

Jarvis ignored Eden's voice on the intercom. He was almost done; he had to talk with Cooper about their new friends. He looked up and the multi-colored ball had led them back almost ten miles already.

He moved the bodies into the camera's blind spot; he knew Cooper was trying to watch him. Jarvis spent that time cutting out two of Strickland's teeth and his hand. It took a little scraping with his knife, but he found gold under the white teeth enamel. His hand didn't have a single bone in it. He was a composite of gold and steel; strong stuff. Once Jarvis had all the blood and skin cleaned off, what remained was a shiny, robotic hand.

The brain was the key. Science had figured out that replacing most of a twenty-third century human warrior. That was an unfortunate part of the gig, you can live with two vat grown or bionic limbs but the brain was different. He afraid there was only one way to find out. Jammer was an android and now he was pretty damn sure Strickland was too.

Did they know? That was just one question he had. The next was, *how long had they been fakes? Since the mission began? Since he captured them? Or longer?* He didn't have any answers but he was pretty sure who did.

A large dragon-bird flew overhead. The water on the inkblots rippled like the surface of a lake under a breeze but they stayed in formation. A second and third dragon-bird flew several miles above. They let out high pitched screams. Jarvis ignored them.

He lifted what was left of Jammer's body up over the rails. The body looked like a thousand-year-old mummy and Jarvis was remorseful. Jammer wasn't like the rest of his team; he wasn't trouble. He was just a daredevil pilot. Each job, he told them, would be his last. Money—and more importantly, excitement—kept bringing him back. This really was his last mission

It wasn't really Jammer. It was a machine.

Pissed, Jarvis pushed the body into the river. He went back and heaved Strickland's body. Heavier, Strickland took a little more effort but he managed to drop the body in the water. It made a fat plopping sound when it landed. He never believed they would die this far from Earth. He fell back on the deck, angry and exhausted as the ship kept chugging away.

A wall of fog now hung to the east side of the river. His heart raced as he realized they were heading toward it. There was no way to know what was on the other side. It was too thick for their sensors to cut through. It might be a waterfall, a wall, or an army of jurassus with battle axes. There was no way to know.

"Fuck it." Jarvis closed his eyes as they entered the fog bank. His skin goose-fleshed as cold air surrounded them. He had been so accustomed to the horrific hot air that followed them everywhere, the cool fog was a relief to his sore body.

"Eden, Cooper, get up here," Jarvis shot the command through their neural net.

Eden was first on deck; she shivered and put her uniform shirt back on unbuttoned over her tank top.

Cooper waved his hand in the fog. "It's freezing."

The fog was so thick you could barely see your hand in front of your face.

"Where are we?" Cooper asked.

"Looks like the Styx River." Jarvis appeared so close to Cooper that the man jumped.

"Not funny." Cooper started back toward the stairs.

Jarvis grabbed his arm. "I wasn't joking."

Cooper pulled his arm back but Jarvis didn't let go.

"Not so fast. Enough of this need-to-know bullshit. Those things said they are taking us to the target, so fess up. Tell us the truth."

Eden stepped close enough that he could see her in the freezing fog.

"Eden, Plan C!" Jarvis barked.

Eden lifted her pistol to Cooper's temple.

"You fucking morons!" Cooper signaled his neural net to ignite the self-destruct sequence. It signaled him back that the system had been disarmed. Jarvis started a mental countdown. It wouldn't be long before Cooper would undo Eden's hack.

"I'll admit it took her awhile to find it, but your doomsday button is not available. I don't care about your target get us off this planet." Jarvis held his pistol steady against Cooper's temple.

Copper started to sweat; he was nervous.

"We're so close Jarvis, look." Cooper pointed beyond them.

Jarvis turned to see the fog had opened up. They were on a tributary at the base of a mountain. A lake appeared in the distance and Jarvis thought he knew that within minutes they would be at their destination. The inkblots spun wildly above them, suddenly going crazy. As they passed through the final portion of the fog, Eden gasped. A huge snow-capped mountain rose before them. The fog had blocked out the immensity of the mountain. The gas giant spun above the peak.

It was a beautiful sight. Smoke from a fire rose up in the distance. The thought of escape melted away at the awe and wonder before them. Jarvis tried to collect his thoughts.

"The target is close?" Jarvis asked.

Cooper nodded. The inkblots continued to spin feverishly

and then took off in every direction. "Was it something I said?" Cooper quipped.

"No more bullshit, Cooper. I know this is Eden, my Eden. I don't know what the others were but they weren't my team." Jarvis focused back on the old man.

Cooper turned and looked at the pistol pointed at his head. Eden kept her gun on Cooper but Jarvis's confusion registered on her face.

"He's distracting you, Nick. stay focused." Eden yelled.

Cooper ignored her. "You should be flattered, Jarvis. I chased the best killer from every human world across centuries. and the fact is I knew who I needed. No one else could do this."

"Oh, that's sweet," Eden said sarcastically and shoved her rifle against his temple, where Jarvis had been pressing his pistol before stepping back. "What the fuck is going on?"

They approached the shoreline of the lake. Cooper rolled his eyes. "We can't get off this planet without my codes to the drop ship. I don't need the self-destruct codes unless you plan on retiring here. "Cooper locked eyes with Nick. "You need to promise no matter how bad it sounds, you'll kill the target."

Jarvis shook his head. "The truth. Nothing less."

"OK, the target was sent here to find and remove any intelligent life that might be here," Cooper explained.

"Genocide? Ecocide?"

"The UN and The Asian Bloc have been fighting up there for decades." Cooper pointed at the sky. "We have nine of Earth's largest cities coming here. The human race needs this planet. Our target was hired to survive, and I didn't lie. Before his team came here, nobody—and I mean no one—had lasted ten minutes. The UN knew about the octopus-things that lived under the ocean."

"That's impossible, before we left the ark, ships hadn't even arrived," said Eden.

"FTL probes had; we knew damn well what was here," Cooper told her.

"How can we trust a word you're saying?" asked Jarvis.

Cooper shrugged and turned away.

"The one that killed Jammer; it said they have cities?" Eden probed.

"Thousands. The target was the first to make contact. He and his survivors went rogue, refused pick up." Cooper explained.

Jarvis thought about it.

Eden's rifle shook slightly in her hand. "The target isn't Garay, is it?"

Jarvis was afraid of what the he was going to say. Cooper opened his mouth to answer.

A dragon-bird scream shattered the silence of the river and rattled the ship.. Eden reflexively dropped her gun and covered her ears, It was the opening Cooper was waiting for. He kicked her against the railing and ran toward the turret-gun. The dragon-bird careened down at them, blocking the sky.

It opened its mouth to swallow Cooper. Eden and Jarvis shot at the beast but it ignored them. Cooper jumped over the railing. Eden reached for him but it was too late. Burnett stepped on to the deck and lifted his rifle. The dragon-bird opened its mouth, taking a mouthful of machine gun fire before swallowing Burnett whole and lifting back into the air.

CHAPTER 31

THE LONG NIGHT came to Tartarus as the moon slipped around to the far side of the gas giant. After the ship passed through the fog bank, the oven-like humidity of the moon had come back. Now, night arrived and the temperature dropped slightly again. After the ship passed the fog belt the oven like humidity of the moon came back. Jarvis and Eden were only aware of the night coming because the AC shut down for the first time in Earth days worth of hours. The dragon-bird had pounded on the shell of the ship for fifteen minutes. It felt like an eternity.

They held each other and waited. Both assumed the dragon-bird would tear the ship open like a can opener. They looked pathetic but there was no one left to posture for. As night fell and the dragon-bird finally flew off, they had the first real silence in over a week of Earth time, Jarvis felt exhaustion for the first time. He closed his eyes and held Eden tight.

Her heart had been racing, but now it slowed. They needed rest. Jarvis used his internal link to the onboard computer to access the external cameras. Nothing moved outside. He signaled the computer to lock all the doors and hatches and closed his eyes. He could still see outside in his neural net. He kissed Eden's forehead. It was greasy from drying sweat.

"Get some sleep," he told her.

Eden looked up at him and he could see her fear. She buried it deep, but it was there. He had trained her how to bury those feelings. She was a tough one from the first time they'd met. Jarvis suddenly felt guilty about Amanda Eden and his effect recruiting her had on her life.

"We need to find Cooper, I'm gonna..." Eden's words died off as Jarvis placed one finger over her lips. He shushed her like a child, and she almost punched him for it. As condescending as it was, the gentle kindness coming from a warrior like Jarvis disarmed her.

"We can't do anything without rest," He told her.

Eden pushed him away. "Stop talking down to me."

Jarvis put up his hands in mock surrender. He knew better than to argue. He hadn't recruited Eden because she was soft. The first time he met her, she was putting 600 pounds of weight on the leg press.

<<< >>>

It was after midnight local time, and she had three days left before a championship match. The gym was empty and she danced between equipment, blasting music that shook the mirrors.

He watched her for a few minutes before she saw him and nearly jumped out of her skin. She used her neural net to cut off the music feed,.

"This is a private gym," she began to argue.

Jarvis shook his head. "Pretty late for a workout."

Eden grabbed a towel and wiped sweat from her forehead. She refused to let him intimidate her. He knew that despite the stripes on his sleeve and the official looking uniform; he only had five years on her.

"Not really, this is Mars. We have a extra forty minutes each day," said Eden without a smile.

"Humanity used to juggle twenty-four time zones. Time is not what it was a hundred years ago," Jarvis told her.

She smiled; it was the first time she smiled at him.

"Just so you know there are almost forty different time being used on earth." She racked the weight. "So you interrupted my workout to talk to me about modern humanity's fractured sense of time?"

Jarvis shook his head. "Pretty lame pick-up line. But that's not why I'm here. Tell me, Amanda, how much do you love gymnastics?"

She laughed. "I'm sorry; you have me at a disadvantage. I didn't catch your name?"

"I didn't give it, but you can call me Jarvis."

One eyebrow went up. "If you're not going to tell me your first name then you'll have to call me Eden."

Jarvis nodded. "It's a beautiful name."

"Give me a break," Eden walked to a weight bench and loaded plates on the bar. "Don't you think your question is a bit personal?"

Jarvis positioned himself to spot her on the flat bench. She had one hundred and seventy-five pounds on the bar. She put up her right hand signaling five reps and Jarvis nodded. He gave her a lift off but she controlled the weight easy. After the fifth, she racked the weight and looked up at him.

"I get the feeling you know I hate it. I mean the gymnastics."

"It seems to be a greater passion for your mother," he conceded.

Eden looked up at him over the bar and laughed. "It was a ticket off Earth; who doesn't want that?"

He couldn't explain why he had chosen her. He saw her compete, and thought she looked beautiful, strong, and intelligent. Beauty and intelligence didn't necessarily matter in a warrior, but they could be useful. He read her file and saw a potential warrior in her.. At first, he just wanted to meet her, but now that he had, he knew he wanted her on the team. He felt a connection, and wanted to be around her. To see that smile every day; to hear her laugh.

The saddest part was he knew Eden joining their squad

would kill any chance at romance. He was taking raw talent and beauty and molding a killer. He did so without remorse but if he was being honest a part of him just wanted to be closer to him. Amanda Eden might as well be a name added to the list of his war crimes.

"Amanda Eden, how would you like to travel to exciting places and be all you can be?" He smiled down at her.

The dumbest pick up line she ever heard, but it worked.

<<< >>>

Now, laying together in the ship, Jarvis looked at her, two pistols on her hips and murder in her eyes. Jarvis cupped her face with his hands.

"I'm sorry," Jarvis said just above a whisper. "I never should have talked to you, that first night."

Eden was confused. "It's a little late to regret that now."

Jarvis turned away, barely containing a rage toward himself.

"You weren't like the rest, I choose them because they were born killers. I just wanted you, and made you into one. A cold-blooded killer, just because I wanted you. I didn't think anyone was capable of loving people like us."

Eden looked away; his strength was one of the things she loved about him. She hated seeing guilt and fear on his face. She knew what she was getting into when she met him.

She turned back to him. "Bullshit, I had a choice. Every killer does. I could blame you Nick, I could blame society. Hell, I've heard you do it enough."

Jarvis shook his head. "I never killed anyone for the hell of it, and I never—"

"Oh great here it comes." She sat up and threw her arms in the air. "You're going to give me civilization's 'Garbage Men' speech. That worked great in training, I was young and impressionable. I believed I was just taking out the trash. Forget it, Nick, I made a choice. I said yes and now I'm here."

Outside, screams broke through the stillness. Jarvis relaxed a little when he realized it was a human scream, and not an approaching dragon-bird. It was someone in pain, suffering, screaming in almost total madness. "You think that's Cooper?" asked Eden as the two of them scrambled out of bed and up to the command center.

Jarvis hit the commands to view the outside cameras on the large screen. Eden sat in the pilot's chair and accessed the sensors directly to her neural net then spun certain cameras and read-outs on the screen in front of them.

"Where is he?" Eden whispered.

He had sounded close. The sensors swept the area repeatedly. The screaming continued, getting closer and louder. There were no signs of life, human or non-human. Eden hit the console.

"Where the fuck is he?" she yelled out of frustration.

"Look for signs of a cloak or masking," he told her.

They found nothing. Unless it was a perfect cloak, there would be some sign of life, even if it were faint. Jarvis checked his pistols and started up the stairs.

"Stay here." Jarvis knew she wouldn't like that. "You're my extra eyes."

Jarvis stepped out on the deck. The turret-gun hung smashed and its spent rounds littered the deck. The only light came from the reflection of the gas giant off the white snow from the mountain. The dark side of Beta filled half the sky, while the other half twinkled with a million pinprick stars. It seemed impossible but even after years of suffering, he found he missed the dead shell of that planet. He wondered which pinprick in the sky was his home star.

The night was impossibly dark and the tortured screams continued. Jarvis held a light with his left hand and under his right hand was a pistol. He followed the sound of the screams to their source along the lake's shore. He heard Eden curse over the intercom as she saw it too.

Burnett walked slowly across the shoreline, his body torn and destroyed. That was the screaming they heard, from the torn and battered body of their once-living teammate. Burnett moved awkwardly and looked chewed up and spit out. One of his arms hung at an unnatural angle. His torso oozed guts and other organs and had been shredded by giant bite marks. Still, he walked.

"I'm not picking up any life signs," Eden called out over the intercom.

"No, I don't suppose you would," Jarvis sighed.

Jarvis turned off the automatic firing and squeezed the trigger. The bullet exploded in Burnett's chest, and his body slumped, but he continued walking toward the ship. Jarvis fired again, this time taking a off a chunk of head. Burnett's body fell back into the lake and floated. It continued to scream as it slowly sunk beneath the water.

"Is he dead?" Eden asked.

"I don't know how to answer that." Jarvis holstered his gun.

The night was silent again. Far off he heard insects clicking and various sounds of the forest. It took a few seconds for it to register, but the sound of the river was gone. The lake was large enough and they had floated far enough into the center of the lake that they no longer heard the flowing river. That noise had been background for so long, Jarvis felt strange without it. For a short moment, it made him uncomfortable, but then he was thankful.

It was a good thing it was quiet, because he might not have heard it otherwise. A small drone landed just behind him. He didn't hear it fly in on silent mode, but he heard it land. Had its surface not been damaged from the dragon-bird's attack, it would have landed silently. It's now-uneven surface tipped it slightly off balance and it made a light tap.

Who ever the target was, wherever they were, they had an eye on them now. Jarvis was about to signal Eden they were being watched when he recalled that Cooper and Garay knew their codes. He knew the drone was moving closer and that it would extend an arm, like a long pinky finger with a camera at the end, to send back images of him to whomever controlled it.

The drone sensed any movement. He turned his head and waited until its arm poked around at him. Jarvis dove and reached for the end of the arm. He grabbed it and flipped it around. The drone smashed on the floor and fired several rounds of automatic fire wildly over his head. Jarvis pulled both his guns free, hoping to destroy the thing before the camera locked on him and gave away his identity.

The drone exploded before he could pull his triggers. Jarvis had to roll away from the shrapnel. Behind the flames, he saw Eden holding a smoking rocket pistol. Jarvis stood up and straightened his uniform. "We have to go before they send another one."

CHAPTER 32

JARVIS PUT ON A CLEAN UNIFORM, one that wired to mask signs of life. He grabbed a pack filled with enough supplies to last them a night or two. Eden slung her rifle over her shoulder and moved quickly to shut down the computers. She coded everything so only she or Jarvis could re-engage the on-board systems. She tried one last time to raise the drop ship to call for a pick-up.

Nothing but static. Jarvis snapped his fingers at her. They jumped off the ship and ran into the woods less than three minutes since torching the drone. Realistically there could have been several drones already hunting them. The woods were thick; the trees were as big as buildings. Despite their size, they swayed under the powerful wind created by the tidal pull of the gas giant planet spinning beyond the atmosphere. The rings of Beta became visible in the southern sky before they got lost in the total darkness of the woods.

Once they were deep enough, Jarvis and Eden switched to night vision contacts. It gave the world an unnatural, overcast day look. When they had them on, they saw a large tribe of jurassus following them. They were the size and build of large silverback gorillas but their dinosaur-like heads snapped at them with anger. None of the smaller members of the tribe were there; Jarvis thought this must be a hunting party.

Jarvis stopped Eden, and the creatures following them came to a halt as well. For now, they kept their distance. He didn't want to fire; it would give away his position. Eden pulled out her knife; he holstered his weapons and unsheathed the large knife he had taken off Strickland's body.

Eden fell back on her training and stood with her back to Jarvis. They watched, knives ready, as the jurassus walked toward them, dragging their knuckles. Jarvis had difficulty with the idea of killing them. They were too much like gorillas, who were revered on Earth like all other species nearly exterminated and ultimately rescued from extinction.

The reality was that to these beings, they were invaders, and for that Jarvis didn't blame them. It was their instinct to attack, and attack they did. One of the largest ran at Eden; she ran to meet him and then slid like she was scoring a game-winning run. She took out its ankles and the creature fell toward Jarvis. Jarvis grabbed the jurassus facing him by its arm and pulled it forward.

The two jurassus slammed into each other with violent force and turned to attack each other. Jarvis jumped over them and took off in the woods behind Eden, who was a faster runner. She hooked his arm through hers and pulled him along. The creatures screamed and some ran in pursuit.

With a quick look back, Jarvis saw the majority stayed to break up the fight. Eden turned and swung the rifle around putting her hand on the rocket launcher and firing one of the gas rockets. The jurassus pursuing them ran off screaming, trying to shake the foul smell off.

"Fuck!" Jarvis grabbed her arm. "We have to move, you just gave away our position."

"I couldn't kill them," Eden wailed.

Jarvis pulled on her but she ripped her arm free as they ran through the woods. They ran far quickly and the sound of the screaming jurassus sounded far off. Jarvis dropped behind a large tree and relaxed, his chest heaving from the run.

Eden looked at him. "Come on, we can't stop now."

Jarvis shook his head. "Maybe we need to try and figure out how to get off this planet."

He needed to tell her everything. Before, he didn't know what to believe, but now he felt he had to trust her. He wasn't sure where to begin: the androids, Zana's body in the camp...he thought about what to say next but she spoke first. "Yeah I agree but we need to find Cooper and kill the target."

Jarvis tried to hide his shock. She had not cared about the target before. He stared at her; she looked unreal in the night vision glare.

"Why the change of heart?" He asked her.

"What the fuck are you talking about?" Her voice rose in anger.

"You didn't care about the target before," Jarvis explained.

Eden considered her words. Jarvis didn't like her calculating look.

"Maybe I didn't, but I also just saw Burnett walking around after some dinosaur-looking thing flew out of the fucking sky and swallowed him. So I'm a little more open minded right now."

They stared each other down for a long time before Jarvis sighed deeply. He reached out for her hand and squeezed. Her hand was soft, almost too soft, and that made him worry too. He still didn't know what to think He smiled, and she returned it. He loved her and he wanted so badly to trust the love returned in her smile.

She put her hand on his cheek. He savored the warmth, but didn't feel comfortable enough to close his eyes.

"We've been in worse spots," Eden said softly.

His eyes got wide. "When?"

She rolled her eyes. "OK, this pretty bad, but we can do this."

She leaned in and kissed him, their lips moving together. He felt her hot breath mingle with his. Her heart beat wildly in her chest as she pulled him close. He couldn't help wonder if that heart was designed in lab and built by machines. For the moment, she felt real enough.

CHAPTER 33

THEY MARCHED through the forest toward the rising smoke. It wasn't long before some put out the fire. Eden calculated the location, they were certain it was a camp less than a kilometer away. They found a stream that flowed from the mountain and they both knew that the target was camped along this stream. That is if the target had the same training as them. They still had water they bottled from the ship but Jarvis realized he had been on this planet for more than a week's worth of hours and hadn't tasted the indigenous water.

The river was disgustingly warm. Strickland had taken a swim in it during their first few hours here, but no one wanted to after getting a feel for the water and certainly no one was jumping at the idea of drinking it.

He whistled softly to Eden and stopped by the stream. He touched it with his finger and despite the overwhelming humidity—even at night—this water was cold. Eden leaned down beside him as he cupped a handful of water. It felt like Earth water, but looked cleaner. He brought to his lips. It didn't have that hot, bubbly feeling that made most of the water on this moon feel different from Earth water, but it tasted more pure.

He swallowed the whole handful down and laughed.

"Must be good?" Eden arched one eyebrow.

Jarvis splashed some on her in response; she laughed and splashed some on him. He laughed and allowed himself to enjoy the moment when he heard a distant sound. He stood up and turned around. Behind them two huge jurassus crept up, hiding behind trees. Maybe they were smarter than they originally thought.

Eden lifted her rifle and walked slowly toward them. Jarvis pointed at her rifle and sent a message to her neural net.

No shooting.

Eden nodded and slung her rifle across her back. They darted behind two trees and Jarvis peeked out to see one of the jurassus doing the same thing – peeking around. He turned and leaned his back against the tree while Eden watched across the lake. Jarvis turned and bit back a shout; the other jurassus stood right in front of him. He swung his knife but he was too late. One giant muscled arm blasted into his chest, knocking him down on to the ground.

He saw the trees above him, but heard Eden's feet shuffle as she ran toward the jurassus. He sat up just in time to see her stab the creature in the rib area. It grunted and grabbed her and she flopped like a ragdoll in its grip. Her face turned red as the large beast squeezed her. Jarvis jumped up and despite the other jurassus galloping toward them, he focused on Eden.

She would be dead in seconds if he didn't act.

He jumped on the creature's vast back. Acting instinctively, he grabbed its massive neck and twisted. Bones snapped, the head twisted, and its vocal cords were crushed, stifling a scream.

Eden gasped and dropped when the jurassus's dead arms let go. Jarvis stepped back and stared at his hands. He was strong, but he didn't think he had that kind of strength. He was still staring at his hands when he heard Eden's rifle hum as the targeting system came to life.

The first jurassus stared at him. A scared and confused look crossed its face as it looked at its dead partner. Jarvis understood its confusion, he was a little thing compared to the enormous animals, and snapped the huge jurassus's neck like a twig.

"Don't shoot," Jarvis whispered to Eden. She held her pistol but didn't fire.

The jurassus hissed and backed off slowly. Eden kept her eye on it as it retreated. Once it was far enough away, the creature turned and ran. Jarvis knew it was getting the rest of the tribe. He pulled on Eden's arm. She stood up and gasped when he saw the dead creature's head spun around unnaturally. "Fuck. How did you kill it?" she asked and looked over at Jarvis. "How did you do that?"

Jarvis ignored her. "The first group as small group, I think we can expect an army next."

Eden grabbed his arm and pointed down at the dead jurassus."How?"

He pulled from her grasp and ran. She only hesitated a few seconds before he heard her footsteps following him.

CHAPTER 34

FOG ROLLED in off the river and across the lake. It looked like it followed them; it wasn't like any Earth fog. It glowed with a light green tint and looked toxic. They stopped; they had reached the foothills of the mountain. The fog continued to follow them, and worse, it lit up the night. Its unnatural glow was enough to show the hiding places of a new creature. A large cat-like animal crawled tightly across the ground toward them. Its body twisted like a snake, but it walked on four short legs. It was a freaky little critter.

Jarvis looked around and gave himself a less than gentle reminder: *you're on a fucked up world that feels nothing like Earth, or any other planet humans want to be on. Kill this fucking target and get off this piece of shit moon.*

Eden wanted to stare at the fog as it rolled up the mountain. Jarvis whistled a short burst that resembled the call of the birds that sang constantly along the river. The whistle got her attention and she joined him.

All talking had moved to messages on their server; they were getting close. They saw sign after sign of human life. Fishing rods left by the stream, traps, and various scanners. They easily tricked and disarmed the sensors. They might not have seen them but they were placed by the book. Not some West Point army crap, no they were placed and coded to a special signal that only ten or so people in the human expanse were ever trained to use.

Jarvis wrote those codes himself, and only his team knew them. To the best of his knowledge, most of those ten people were dead or had been replaced by machines.

He admitted to himself it was probably Garay. One of his own personal monsters, he taught him everything he knew and yet the man had managed to learn so much more. That should mean killing him should be easy, but if any one of his monsters excelled in improvisation, Garay was the one. There was one other possibility, one he couldn't wrap his mind around.

A copy. How many copies were out there?

Eden slowed her steps and walked with a quieter touch. She must have heard something. Jarvis checked the numbers on his uniform; his cloak signal was still strong. Once they were twenty clicks from the campfire he would expect hundreds of sensors. They had to shut them down, replace them with self-replicating false signals.

Jarvis knew the codes. If Garay was watching the telemetry he would know they turned off the sensors as long as he wasn't staring at the read-out during the three seconds it took to rewire the network with false readings.

The tricky part was that it would crash their nets too, and for the thirty seconds it took Eden and Jarvis to reboot their nets and scan for viruses, they would be technologically naked, fighting natural as they called it in basic training. Jarvis was a twenty-third century warrior and the last thing he wanted to do was go into battle in his birthday suit.

Eden signaled him to get down and they ducked behind a large fallen tree. As Jarvis dropped, he saw it. The camp consisted of a tent, an unlit fire pit, and a half-constructed cabin. They were crouched about fifty yards up the ridge from the camp, but close enough that he could hear the cloth of the tent flap in the wind.

His cloak read-out signaled his net. His contact lenses

flashed the location of the sensors in his eye-sight. There were hundreds of scanners and the cloak was cycling false readings. It wouldn't work much longer; a uniform cloak only had so many false signals. They had to re-set the sensors. He was ready. If it gave away their presence, the only brightside is their target would attack and it would give them a chance to identify him.

We have to re-set the sensors now.

Eden nodded. They had to do it together. With so many sensors they had to send out just the right set of signals. They would use the cloak to send out a burst of enough false-life signs; enough to populate twenty-first century China. That would overload their nets but it would do the trick.

The signals went out. Jarvis forgot the sharp intensity of it, like an ice pick drilling slowly into the side of his head. He grabbed Eden's backpack and pulled out a scope that hooked on top of his right hand pistol. He poked over the fallen tree. Eden rubbed her temples in pain when the grid-sensors went down. She reached for her rifle as Jarvis scanned the campsite.

He looked though the high-powered scope. He had to turn off night vision because it overwhelmed his contacts. The tent opened on the far side and someone walked out wearing the same uniform Jarvis issued to all his squad. Too small to be Garay, whoever it was and he wore a hat. Jarvis had the crosshairs of the scope firmly centered on the man's back, and Jarvis thought about the trigger. The rifle was more accurate.

"Eden quick," he whispered.

The target turned around and it was like looking in a mirror. Under the hat, now running in their direction, was a man who looked exactly like Nick Jarvis.

Eden lifted herself up using the rifle as a crutch. Jarvis tried to push her back; he didn't want her to see. A bullet exploded over their heads. He had given away their position. He pushed her down and away at the same time. His net server tried to connect with his wetware links as bullets exploded around them.

Eden turned, lifting her rifle as their target jumped on top of the tree that had been their sanctuary. She pointed the rifle at her arm's length, an easy shot. Her eyes locked on the target and Jarvis watched her turn white. Another Nick Jarvis pointed two pistols at them and he froze in shock. Jarvis yanked at Eden and pulled and nearly broke her arm. With his other hand, he fired back at the target, which he now realized was himself: Target-Jarvis. The tree exploded into shards. Target-Jarvis dived away from them, firing both pistols.

The forest exploded into chaos. Jarvis let go of Eden's arm. He twisted and felt someone tackle him. He rolled and came up pointing both pistols on himself; well, Target-Jarvis. The target had lost his hat, and they wore the same uniform. They stared at each other in shock and disbelief. They were identical; a perfect copy. Then he heard a voice that sounded exactly like his.

"Eden? Oh my god," Said Target-Jarvis.

Jarvis couldn't take his eyes off the target but sensed Eden watching them.

"Don't you fucking talk to her!" Jarvis shouted.

"What the fuck?" Eden yelled and pulled away from both of them. Jarvis heard her footsteps crunching on the ground as she ran off into the jungle.

The two Jarvises held their guns high and stared at each other. Target-Jarvis spoke first.

"Well, now things are getting interesting."

CHAPTER 35

JARVIS SLOWLY PUSHED himself off the ground and then took a step back in the direction Eden had run. Target-Jarvis remained still but held his gun steady.

"I think we need to talk," said Target-Jarvis.

Jarvis kept both pistols pointed at him, so did his clone. "You don't really think I am gonna trust a fucking word you say, do you?"

"Well you came here to kill me, right?" Target-Jarvis grinned. "Despite that, I'm still willing to talk." He shrugged.

Jarvis felt his arms getting sore, but he couldn't drop them, not now. "OK, Talk."

Target-Jarvis stood still but his eyes scanned Jarvis. It's what he would do—look for weakness.

"Let's start with who sent you and how many did you come with?" Target-Jarvis asked.

Jarvis grinned. "The UN sent me, and I'm not a moron."

Target-Jarvis looked over his shoulder. "She looks just like her, beautiful. Does she know?"

"Know what?"

"The whole squad is dead, I'm the only one who made it this far."

Jarvis shook his head. "Yeah, about that. I saw your handiwork back at the desert camp. Zana?"

Target-Jarvis closed his eyes for split second and Jarvis almost pounced, but the anguish on Target-Jarvis's face disarmed him.

"I took care of Garay. He was crazy," Target-Jarvis whispered.

Jarvis ignored him and what his comment meant. He continued trying to send messages over to Eden's server, but it was offline. He had to find her.

"They claimed Garay was the target, right?" said Target-Jarvis, shaking his head. "He was just bait, I knew they wouldn't copy him. Too unpredictable."

Jarvis wasn't listening to him; he was worried about Eden.

Target-Jarvis saw his confusion. "I wouldn't be so worried about her, she's just a robotic copy. Human Eden is dead. I promise you that."

"Bullshit," Jarvis stepped back quickly. "You're a rogue clone, an android copy sent to fuck with my head."

"Have you considered for one minute that you're a Merc-droid?"

Jarvis laughed, "A what?"

"Mercenary-Android copy. It's not as crazy as it sounds. In the twenty-third century back home, it was impossible. This system of worlds, this century, is a whole new ball game. What do you think they were doing with our bodies the whole time we slept?"

Jarvis shook his head. Target-Jarvis stepped closer.

"Think about it. I'm one tough son-of-a-bitch, hard to kill; I have a team of hard-to-kill motherfuckers under my command. Who else are you going to copy?"

"Stop! This is bullshit. I know who I am."

"Family right? Sammy was my son. They gave you my memories too; after all, if you think you're human, you'll act like one—for better or worse." Target-Jarvis shrugged his shoulders.

Jarvis laughed, squeezing the grip on his pistols. "My family is dead; have been for hundreds of years now."

Target-Jarvis squinted, considering it.

"OK," Target-Jarvis kept his cool. "DNA copies, now that is easy shit. They had me in a sleep chamber for years, plenty of time to map my brain."

Jarvis pushed his right pistol forward. "Not you!"

Jarvis pulled the trigger but Target-Jarvis moved quickly and the bullets bounced off his energy shield. The shield blocked the bullets but it buzzed out after a few seconds.

Target-Jarvis dove and rolled behind a tree.

Jarvis took off into the woods. Behind him, he heard Target-Jarvis scream. "They fed you memories, motherfucker!"

Jarvis kept running but heard the voice behind him.

"I am Nick Jarvis!"

CHAPTER 36

"EDEN!" Jarvis yelled as he ran down the hill following her signal.

A bullet snapped on the trail inches behind his feet. Three more followed and he turned to see Target-Jarvis running and firing on his tail. As Jarvis cut into the woods, he turned and shot wildly. Jarvis dropped and changed directions. He crawled through the muck. Target-Jarvis began to fire every three seconds.

"Tell her what you are!" Target-Jarvis yelled. He fired again, counted to three and fired again.

Jarvis knew the pattern; he used it on Titan once to smoke out a competing mercenary hiding in an engineered forest, one not nearly as dense as this. Target-Jarvis would keep firing to unnerve the subject of the search and he would move after each shot so as not to give away his location.

It didn't just look like him and sound like him, but the fucking thing thought like him too.

The firing continued. When Jarvis thought it sounded further away, a blast would snap through the trees above him. He kept crawling, the moist humidity soaking his uniform. He hugged the ground and crawled and suddenly, the ground rumbled. It sounded like a bomb went off in the distance.

The shooting stopped. Jarvis crawled quicker.

A closer explosion rocked the ground harder. A creature he had never seen before ran and leapt over Jarvis and a whole pack of them followed the first up the mountain. The trees shook above him, raining sharp pine needles. They stuck into his uniform, making him look like a porcupine. Jarvis shook them free and rolled on his back. He looked up and the ground shook again. He heard the whistle just before the next boom.

Moon rain; they were passing through the rings.

The ground and trees shook enough to upset his stomach and rattle his fillings. It didn't feel solid ground under him; it felt like he was dropping into atmosphere on an ancient space vessel. He stood and spun 180 degrees, looking up as the burning rocks burned through the sky. One tore through the tree tops above him, hitting the forest at thousands of kilometers per hour. The flaming object passed through the forest as though it were a thin veil of paper, lighting the trees like funeral pyres. The closest moon debris plowed through the forest and hit the stream flowing down the mountain with an incredible force.

Jarvis closed his eyes, felt the intense heat, and waited to die.

It was hot, daylight hot. Jarvis struggled to open his eyes. It was bright, daylight bright. The muddy soil felt like it was just shy of coming to boil. Jarvis's his skin burned raw. His eyes couldn't quite open and he resigned himself to die. A part of him knew damn well it wasn't daylight.

"What the fuck?" A jolt flowed through Jarvis at the sound of Eden's voice. He sat up and found her pointing one of his own pistols on him. Jarvis subconsciously reached for his holsters and finding them empty. They should only respond to his DNA, Eden looked confident as if she had hacked the onboard chip.

"They aren't there." She told him.

The other pistol was tucked in her belt next to her exposed belly button. Entire sections of her uniform were torn and burned away. It might have looked sexy, if her skin wasn't burned down to muscle in spots. She looked oddly calm. Jarvis tried to take a deep breath but the burning forest scorched his lungs and set off a wave of coughs. The forest burned in every direction. The moon rain had ended but the entire south side of the mountain burned around them.

"Eden, thank god." Jarvis put out his hand expecting her to pass over the pistol. She shook her head. Jarvis closed his eyes for second and tamped down his anger. He opened his eyes and held his hand out. She didn't budge.

"What the fuck is happening, Jarvis?" She demanded.

"Nick...My name is Nick."

Eden's arm shook slightly, just enough to show him how off balance she was. "Don't play games. Not now."

Jarvis laughed. "Games? You're pointing my guns at me."

She seemed truly confused; he watched her silently consider giving him his gun back. Her arm stiffened.

"I don't know who you are." Eden told him. "I don't know what you are."

She made a good point..He watched her run and let her have a good minute or two lead. He was confident she was following the stream back to their ship. When the moon rock slammed in the stream it should have killed a normal person. Even at his distance it overwhelmed him. It took him a minute to avoid debris and catch up her prone on the ground.

Jarvis scanned her body. Her legs were torn and bleeding, her stomach was burned like an overcooked slab of meat, her arms were wrecked. Her beautiful face was covered in black oily soot and her hair was singed and gray in places. It was a miracle she still stood, let alone managed to hold a gun on him.

"Two very good questions my dear." Anger peppered his words. She took a step back from him. She had his firearms yet he still struck fear in her; he could feel it. Jarvis stood slowly fighting through a hundred aches and pains.

"Stay down!" Her voice was saturated with fear. He stood.

"He programmed you, you never loved me," Jarvis told her.

More confusion, she shook her head. "No, that's not true. I always loved you."

He couldn't believe those words. It was programming. Somewhere in a lab, a mission specialist told an engineer to write some code in some fucked up complicated computer language. She was wired to love him. That's why even when he made her angry, she couldn't wait to fuck him. She couldn't help herself; it was the program, plain and simple.

"You're a fucking machine!" he screamed at her.

Eden's jaw dropped. She put her left hand on her chest. "Me? I saw you, another you. You're the machine!" Her lip quivered.

"I know what I am," Jarvis stepped forward.

Eden extended her arm, pushing his pistol closer to his chest. Her hand shook.

He spoke softly. "You can't do it."

"I don't know what you are," she whispered.

He realized he had to use her programming against her. It was his only hope.

"You love me, no matter what I do," Jarvis told her.

She shook her head; he saw a tear well up in her eye. He spoke with the same gentle tone he used when they made love.

"Eden." He reached out a hand.

Her finger moved away from the trigger by a hair. Jarvis reached up and grabbed her arm, pulling her forward. She fired wide. He pulled his other pistol out of her belt loop and slammed it up under her chin. Eden lifted into the air before hitting the ground with a dull thud. She screamed and squirmed, trying to grab for her own pistol. She had it in her hand but his boot smashed down on it. The bones and metal in her hand cracked. It wasn't enough to knock the pistols free. She looked up and Jarvis had a pistol pointed at her.

Eden rolled on the ground, looking up at the burning trees around him as they lit up the night. She was going to shoot, he could feel it. Training took over; he didn't even have time to think about it; he squeezed the trigger.

The bullet exploded through her chest and out her back. The bullet had barely left her and Jarvis screamed. Her face contorted in pain but she died instantly. Jarvis dropped his guns and caught her body before it fell.

Warm blood ran over his arms. She struggled for breath, her lips just inches from his ear.

"No, no Nick, no Nick."

He hugged her tight until his hands came across the gaping wound in her back. His heart broke as if someone smashed it with a hammer. He dropped her and looked at the warm fresh blood on his hands. It felt human.

CHAPTER 37

JUST BEYOND HIS BLOOD-COVERED HANDS, Jarvis stared at Eden's body. Her beautiful hazel eyes stared up at the burning forest. Despite the snapping and cracking of trees, her eyes never blinked. It was as sure as any other sign that she was gone.

He closed his eyes and replayed the mission in his head. He thought about every moment he spent with her, trying to determine if there any clue that led him to the truth. He thought about his son and his wife who he left behind and thought of the second chance he had, with Eden. There was no third chance. He threw one gun at the approaching fire and screamed.

His throat burned with the smoke and it matched his uncontrolled fury. He punched himself repeatedly, furious at himself for getting them into this.

The tears and burning anger were unstoppable. He looked away from her body, but the feeling remained. *He had to know if he had been right.*

Jarvis rolled her body over and hesitated. The skin was charred on her arm, and bleeding. He holstered his remaining gun and pulled out his knife. He held her hand. It was still warm and moist with blood, sweat, and tears. He gripped it tightly and began to slice away at the burned skin on her arm.

The muscle was cooked but ripped off with a tug. The blood-stained bone was white underneath—not silver or gold.

It could be some kind of enamel. He scraped at it with his knife. It flaked somewhat but he saw no sign of anything under. He looked up at her blank, dead face. He didn't like what he was thinking. The flames spread toward her body and if he didn't do this now he would never have another chance.

He couldn't live with himself if he didn't know.

She was a fucking machine and he knew it. It didn't matter what he did to that body. It was a machine that fucked him to control him. When he looked at the torn remains of Strickland's body, he knew the machine was a copy in every way except one thing—the operating system, which was inside the toughest part of the body, the skull.

He knew what he had to do.

Jarvis pulled out his gun and spun it around and gripped it by the barrel. He delicately touched the bottom of the steel handle to her forehead to determine the spot he needed. His breath got heavier as he held the weapon against her beautiful face. There was no other way to know, and she was already dead.

He lifted the gun high in the air and froze. *He had to know.* He slammed the gun, butt-down. He closed his eyes and heard a crack. He couldn't open his eyes; he just prayed to a god he never believed in before that he wouldn't miss.

He screamed, sobbed, and slammed the gun again.

Crack!

The slow sound of blood dripping followed. Jarvis whimpered for the first time in his adult life and resisted opening his eyes. He turned away and slowly peeled open one eye. He could just make out her face. It was torn open; the skull broken apart with a nasty looking crack down the middle. Blood poured free.

That didn't mean anything, Jarvis told himself, androids bleed. They bleed a lot. Still partially turned away and only looking peripherally, he ran his finger along the edge of her open skull. Trying to separate the pieces so he could look inside. Too much of her skull remained.

Jarvis thought about Mars, the farm she suggested. The real Eden gave him a chance to run off to a farmstead on Mars. None of this would have happened if he had pulled his head out of his ass and admit how he was feeling back then. He loved her! The real Amanda Eden, not this carbon copy bullshit.

"Fuck you, whatever you are!" Jarvis yelled and spat.

Jarvis screamed as he slammed the pistol down again. This time he didn't pause at the cracking sound. He lifted and dropped the gun over and over, pounding the head repeatedly until he didn't feel anything hard underneath. There was nothing left but soft, wet tissue. Pieces of a broken and destroyed human brain dripped off the handle of his gun.

Below him, the wreckage of Eden's head stared back at him with eyes separated by a cavern of gore. His entire body shook as he moved the barrel of the gun around inside her head looking for anything robotic. There was nothing artificial there and Jarvis felt something snap inside him. Sanity was too narrow a term to explain what he'd lost. He was about to snap when—

"What the have you done you dumb piece of shit." Anger and sorrow mixed on Target-Jarvis's face. "They mixed us up."

Jarvis looked up and saw Target-Jarvis standing one hundred feet away, silhouetted by the fire behind him. All Jarvis could do was scream. Target-Jarvis was on his punching with fury. They rolled on the ground, Target-Jarvis getting him by the throat.

Jarvis shook his head. "Your fault, you're not even human." He struggled to speak through the grip around his neck.

"Just because she was human doesn't mean you are," Target-Jarvis drawled.

Jarvis reached to his right and felt his pistol. He lifted it and fired and pieces of Eden's brain splattered on his face. Target-Jarvis leapt away into the fire. Jarvis roared like an injured lion and fired ten wasted bullets into the flames.

CHAPTER 38

JARVIS FELL over Eden's body. He couldn't look at the wreckage of her face, just clutched her torso and balled like a baby. He roared, screamed, and cursed but it was all a horrific blur. He couldn't get her back, it was over.

The flames danced closer and the heat overwhelmed the coolant in his uniform. Sweat dropped with his tears on to Eden's charred stomach. The flames came for her; he couldn't do anything to save her body. *You killed her goddamn it, you killed her, you mutilated her body; why get sentimental now?*

Unable to continue looking at her head, Jarvis picked up his remaining pistol. He checked it, over four hundred self-replicating rounds. Eden's gun lay on the ground. He picked that up too.

This was not his fault. The man responsible was Cooper, and the fucking copy out there pretending to be him. He looked at Eden's gun, four hundred and fifteen rounds. He figured he had about eight hundred chances to make this right. With that in mind he looked straight at Eden's body, he refused to accept the blame, he needed to keep that imagine in his head and use the anger against his enemy.

Jarvis followed Target-Jarvis into the flames. He burst through and rolled to put out the flames that caught him. With both guns held ready, he ran past the embers of dead trees and cut into the small stream, the only place where the flames had not overtaken the land. Target-Jarvis was in the stream, a few hundred yards up, wading his way towards the lake.

Jarvis fired a shot that clipped Target-Jarvis in his shoulder. It knocked Target-Jarvis back but he fell to the far shore and unslung a rifle. Jarvis jumped behind an ancient tree burning over his head. A rocket burst into it. The red-hot splinters rained down on Jarvis and he used a nearby fallen tree as cover to crawl with intense speed to shoreline.

He lay on his stomach and fired shot after shot at his copy. Target-Jarvis dropped below the water line. Jarvis holstered one of the pistols. If the situations were reversed he would not hide, he would go on the offensive. Suddenly, Target-Jarvis jumped out of the stream in front of him. Jarvis only had a second to jab and knock the rifle out of his copy's hands.

Target-Jarvis was unnaturally strong, but a thanks to days in the heavy gravity of this planet, so was Jarvis. They struggled for control of Jarvis's pistol, which had fallen with a plop into the stream. Both men grunted and tried to overpower the other. They had plenty of time to stare into each other's eyes. Jarvis could see his target was disturbed by the mirror image, an insane version of himself.

"It's your fault," Jarvis said, struggling.

Target-Jarvis shook his head. "I didn't bash her fucking brains in—you did."

Jarvis roared and picked up Target-Jarvis by his throat, twisting him around and slamming him onto the wet, hot soil. Target-Jarvis laughed as Jarvis placed his last pistol under his copy's chin. Target-Jarvis was neither scared or upset.

"Wait!" exclaimed Target- Jarvis. "Before you shoot, you need to think about this."

Jarvis froze. "Where is Cooper? Damn it, I know your working together."

Target-Jarvis grinned. "You're malfunctioning. Have you thought about what you're going to do after you shoot?"

Jarvis pushed the gun harder against his chin. He was afraid to shoot, what if nothing but brains blew out of the top of his clone's head? What would that mean? Target-Jarvis nodded, knowing what Jarvis was thinking.

"Good, slow down. Think carefully. You can blow them out of my head but all you're going to find is brain. Then what?" Target-Jarvis said.

This was the trick; bullshit to make him question himself. This machine knew what it was and Jarvis wasn't going to fall for it.

"Shut the fuck up," Jarvis tensed, ready to kill. "You're a machine."

Target- Jarvis laughed. "Maybe I am, maybe you are."

Jarvis shook slightly. Fear and anger wrecked him inside. Target-Jarvis smiled and kicked up into his opponent's balls. Jarvis clinched up and fired at the dirt, inches from his target's head. Jarvis gripped the pistol as another foot hit his stomach, knocking him back into the stream.

The stream carried him for a few feet before he stood up and pointed the gun. Target-Jarvis was gone. It took him a few moments to orientate himself but he saw the target running along the bank of the stream. He fired several shots. One clipped Target-Jarvis in the leg, but the man weaved in and out of the flames. Target-Jarvis was confusing the heat sensors in his net.

Jarvis stood still in the warm water. He didn't have to guess, there was only one place for them to escape. He was going back to the ship. He had a feeling that was where Cooper waited for him.

CHAPTER 39

JARVIS WAS AN EXCELLENT TRACKER; it was rare that he lost a target, and never one bleeding from his leg. He had to assume that his copy knew that. Target-Jarvis cut a crisscross path across the burning forest. When Jarvis let his copy get away, he hoped that the target would assume he was so unstable that his skills were diminished.

In reality his skills were sharp; he found the trail of blood but ignored it. If his copy thought like him, he would cut around the forest taking his time, making it look like he was heading back to camp. The camp was encircled by fire and crushed by moon debris, so Target-Jarvis wouldn't go back there. Jarvis walked calmly along the bank of the river. He used his neural net to scan for signals; he found the central computer on the ship was working, which meant Cooper was already there. He was the only one who could override the code Eden left on the AT's computer.

The flames died out as he got closer to the lake and the ship. Once the ship was visible, he dropped to the ground and crawled, setting his uniform to camouflage. He also sent out cloak signals. Since he programmed the ship's sensors he knew the codes and approached with a perfect cloak.

Considering the firestorm he just escaped the lake looked

placid and calm. The unnatural green fog still hung just over the lake, lighting the area. The ship's engine hummed away as Jarvis moved closer. Two searchlights scanned the ground at the shoreline from Cooper's drones floating above the ship.

Jarvis pulled out a mini-drone from his pocket; it was the size of his middle finger. He flipped the safety on his pistol and shook the mini-drone it until it glowed dully. Next he inserted the drone into the end of his pistol, pulled the trigger, and launched it. A tiny *pssst* noise floated past his ear as it left the barrel. Jarvis picked up its location and guided it a kilometer away. He sent it up a ridge closer to the edge of the forest fire. Once the mini-drone slowed down, he drove it into the ground where it broke like a branch under a foot.

The mini-drone broadcasted fake life signs from its position. The drones on the ship darted off like missiles. It confirmed what he suspected: they were looking for him. Jarvis stood up and ran to the ship's hull. He only had a few more seconds before Cooper re-configured the cameras. Jarvis climbed up the rope ladder and dove and rolled across the deck.

He jumped and grabbed the roof on the center section of the ship. He grunted at the effort but flipped himself on to the roof, just in time. His neural net signaled that the cameras had adjusted. He laid flat on the roof of the ship.

The large drones flew to the spot where the mini-drone led them and once he saw them land in position, he sent out the signal. It was a pulse of energy that overloaded the on-board direction control. Within seconds the command center lost their sensor signal.

"Goddamn it!" Jarvis faintly heard Cooper curse from inside the ship. The mini-drone's battery was dying; it was only designed for approximately five minutes of operation and he already pushed it beyond it's specs. It lifted into the air and Jarvis saw the image he was waiting for.

Target-Jarvis was running toward the ship. The image blinked out as the drone self-destructed. Jarvis heard Cooper run out on to the deck. Cooper put a bullet into a chamber; judging from the sound it was an automatic rifle.

"Hold it right there!" Cooper yelled.

"Easy, easy it's me," said Target-Jarvis.

Cooper harrumphed. "And which 'me' is that?"

Jarvis couldn't risk looking over the edge, but from the sound of his voice it seemed that Target- Jarvis wasn't more than twenty feet from the boat. He watched the strange, swirling bright green fog and listened to them argue.

"I'm Nick Jarvis. You brought me here to kill a target, and it might have been nice if you told me it was my clone."

The bastard is pretending to be me. Jarvis felt a fresh wave of anger.

"Clone? Not exactly." Cooper cleared his throat. "You could still be the target."

"He killed Eden." There was a little sadness in Target-Jarvis's voice. Not much, just enough.

"And I killed him," Target-Jarvis continued. "Mission accomplished."

Unbelievable, Jarvis thought. He had to act soon.

Jarvis pulled a small mirror out of his pocket and held it up at an angle so he could watch his copy. Target-Jarvis stood there without a gun, as far as Jarvis could see. His hands were raised and he had a knife in his right hand. If Target- Jarvis skills equal to Jarvis, he could take out Cooper with that knife almost as fast as he could with a gun.

"Is that so?" Cooper continued. "Which member of the team died here first?"

Target-Jarvis didn't know what to say. In the mirror Jarvis saw the muscle in Target-Jarvis's knife arm tightening. He was about to attack. Cooper lifted his rifle and Target-Jarvis threw the knife overhand. Jarvis rolled off the roof and fired three shots, but Target-Jarvis was already out of sight.

Cooper fell on the deck and dropped his rifle. Jarvis saw the knife stuck in his shoulder. It would hurt but not kill him; Jarvis pulled the knife free and Cooper screamed. Jarvis heard feet land on the deck at the far side of the ship, by the turret-gun. Jarvis looked up, gripping his pistol. That turret-gun was big enough to tear right through the command center. The massive gun exploded, bullets tearing through everything as Jarvis spun on the deck to avoid the fire.

A bullet ripped through his shoulder; another blew a chunk of skin and muscle off his thigh. Jarvis crawled across the deck towards Cooper. As Jarvis crawled closer to him, another line of rapid-fire bullets cut a path across the deck and exploded against both of Cooper's kneecaps. The man screamed as the shots tore his legs in half.

Jarvis laid his hand on Cooper, violently shaking his body as he his pistol back across the deck. Target-Jarvis hid behind the bulk of the turret-gun and Jarvis's shots bounced with flashes against the gun's steel frame. Jarvis hooked his hand under Cooper's shoulder and half pulled, half pushed him toward the stairs. The screaming man reached uselessly for his legs and the trail of blood that followed them.

Once in the stairwell Jarvis pushed him upright, ignoring the fresh waves of pain radiating from his own shoulder. He propped Cooper up at the top of the stairs. They were both breathing heavy and bleeding. Cooper was turning white and blood streamed out of his stumps like two pumps. Jarvis slammed the door shut, leaving a bloody smear of his own. A waterfall of blood dripped down the stairs to pool at the bottom. It all looked messy and very human. Despite the pain, Jarvis was relieved at that thought.

Cooper's eyes closed slowly. Jarvis slapped him.

"Fuck!" Cooper spit blood.

"No dying on me now you fucker," Jarvis told him.

Cooper shook his head with what little strength he had. "Which one are you?"

"That is a very good fucking question," Jarvis laughed.

Cooper tried to get his focus back. "Which one died first?"

"Cason, but he didn't stay dead." Jarvis didn't miss a beat.

Cooper tried to smile but the pain was too great.

"You have to kill him. I called the drop ship. Only I can fly it." Cooper closed his eyes again.

Bullets beat through the stairwell, ripping through the walls like paper. One whizzed over their heads and blew a hole into the door. Cooper wasn't flying anyone anywhere, and Jarvis knew it. The shots stopped. Jarvis shook Cooper again, it took effort the old man didn't have to keep his eyes open.

"What is he? Why did you bring us here? No bullshit!" Jarvis demanded. He had to know what was really going on.

Cooper slid to one side, his eyes rolling back in his head. Jarvis shook him again, cursing. Jarvis punched the wall. This was his last chance to learn the truth.

Something slammed into the door. Target-Jarvis was trying to force it open. The turret-gun must have finally run out of bullets. Jarvis put his pistol barrel right up to the steel door and fired. The shot was loud and tore a hole in the door, but Target-Jarvis had already moved away.

Jarvis ran down the stairs, firing behind as he ran into the armory. He slammed the door and heard his copy coming down the stairs.

"Nowhere to run now!" the copy screamed as he punched the door.

Jarvis looked around the room, most of the weapons had been checked out to the now-dead members of his team. He couldn't escape.

"Everyone is dead but me and my shadow," Jarvis whispered to himself. Anger and rage overwhelmed him. Bullets poured into the room. Target-Jarvis must have picked up Cooper' rifle. Jarvis knew he had to end this: it might not have been rational but Jarvis was one hundred kilometers past rational.

"Hey, clone!" Target-Jarvis yelled through the door. "I'm going to make you pay. You killed Eden you son of bitch!"

Jarvis backed away from the door, shaking his head. That explained his anger, if the situation were reversed and he had watched someone bash in Eden's head...*It wasn't my fault, I was tricked.* Jarvis reminded himself.

"It's your fault, it's Cooper's fault, both of you!" Jarvis yelled.

A fist slammed into the door.

"She loved me," screamed Target-Jarvis.

Jarvis laughed. "You're fucking crazy; she loved me. Nick Jarvis. I'm not a clone, or a fucking android. I'm a man, born to a mother; not some bio-sack in a fucking lab." Jarvis remembered the last mission he gave Eden when he had held her hand in his. He co'uld almost feel it the memory was so strong. He went to the locker that had Cooper's name on it. Eden had been the one to point out that Cooper never opened it. The new passcode Eden made after she broke into the locker and reprogrammed it.

"Think about it," Target-Jarvis yelled through the door. "He fired on me because he knew I'm the real Nick Jarvis. I'm the target, because I'm the template," Target-Jarvis's voice had taken on a conversational tone.

Jarvis ignored him and opened the locker. A duffel bag Cooper had brought from the base ship was propped inside. Unzipping it, Jarvis found the nuke that served as Cooper's back-up self-destruct device. Red, black, and green cables were pulled out to disarm the device.

"They used me to create the perfect killing machine. You think like me, you think you ARE me; the difference is you're faster and stronger. Don't kid yourself, it's not the planet, it's you." Target-Jarvis fired another two-dozen rounds into the room. One hit Jarvis in the back. He fell over; the bullet burned through his body. The pain was good—it felt human. He gripped the three cords to the nuke and stared at them. If he re-connected them it would instantly arm itself.

"You are the machine!" Target-Jarvis yelled through the door. "Through all that rage, you know it's true."

He could be right. He might be the fake. He hadn't wanted to shoot Eden, but instinct took over. Instinct? Or program-ming? Sorrow, rage, and guilt flowed through him. All he knew was neither one of them—neither he nor the clone—deserved to live.

"Fuck you!" Jarvis yelled, pushing the cords into the bomb casing. It instantly came alive. Lights flashed and it emitted a high pitch noise. He was ready. The bomb exploded with the power of a super nova.

CHAPTER 40

HIS EYELIDS FELT HEAVY. It was an odd feeling. The bomb had ignited and then there was nothing, like he was being pushed down into sleep. The feeling didn't last long as he opened his eyes. A light as bright as the sun over-powered his vision. It took a second to adjust; when he did he could tell he was inside a hypersleep chamber.

It's hatch slid open. A clean, fully dressed Cooper stood on solid legs over the chamber. Jarvis sat up sweating and looked around. The bomb had gone off; he felt it. He had embraced it.

The other hypersleep racks opened. Cooper smiled his shit-eating grin. Jarvis watched, stunned, as Eden, Cason, Zana, Weddle...the whole goddamn squad stood up and started stretching.

"What happened?" Jarvis whispered to Cooper.

"Welcome to Beta Tanius," Cooper replied.

Jarvis looked at his hands. He felt uncomfortable in his body. It felt solid; there was no gunshot in his shoulder or his back. He shook his head.

"What do you mean, welcome?" Jarvis looked back up at Cooper.

"Yeah, I told you technology improved. Leaps and bounds

in the last days and months." Cooper looked around at the others as he spoke.

Jarvis remembered him saying the same thing only days ago. This wasn't déjà vu, this was something more fucked up and unexplainable.

Eden moved quickly across the room, Zana looked afraid. Cason tried to hide his fear.

"I thought we were cooked," Jammer said and then laughed. "I didn't even realize we were asleep." It was manic, nervous laughter.

Jarvis jumped down to the deck. The cold steel felt solid under his bare feet. He waited for his legs to give out or feel weak. He rotated his shoulder, no wound at all.

"I have good news," Cooper smiled warmly. "The mission to Tartarus is called off, you have new orders."

Jarvis shook his head. "No, fuck this, it's bullshit."

"Colonel!" Cooper yelled.

Jarvis pointed at him. "No," Jarvis jumped at him. Cooper pushed him into the next room. Jarvis suddenly felt no control over his body. It was like he was a video and Cooper had paused him. He tried to move, he thought about it, but his body didn't respond. Cooper paced in front of him with his hands behind his back.

"You gave us quite a scare, Colonel," Cooper told him.

"You're a machine," Jarvis spit. He saw him die in the blast.

Cooper moved closer and spoke softly so only Jarvis could hear him. "I am your boss, and while it didn't go quite as planned, your first mission was a success. There are several inhabited moons in the Beta system, the new frontier of humanity. While the Asian Bloc controls a lot of the real estate here, the UN is powerful. You will be its muscle."

Jarvis quit struggling, he had zero control over his body. "What am I?"

"What you are is not important. There is a cold war going on here in the system surrounding Beta Tanius. You're Nick

Jarvis, commander of the Goddamn Killing Machines and right now there is nothing else you need to know."

ACKNOWLEDGMENTS

First and foremost my wife Cari for putting up with the hours I spend on other planets, My Dickheads co-hosts Larry and Anthony who have supported this novel and all the others since I have known them. Christoph and Leza at CLASH Books for the hard work and coming through on promises! Edward Morris for reading an early draft, Desmond of Dread Media, James Reich, Brian Evenson, Cody Goodfellow, Gina Ranalli, Ivan Doric, Jeff Burk, Rose O'Keefe , Carlton Mellick III, Justine at Verbatim books, Rob at Mysterious Galaxy bookstore, Brian Keene, Charles Hickey (for a great edit on a chapter I ended up cutting ha-ha.), James Chambers, Brian Asman, Mister Frank at Bizzong, Ryan C Thomas, Chad Stroup, Robert Essig, and Killian. Dan Zigler, Duncan Barlow, Good Clean Issa, Even Lampe, Marissa VU, Jessie at SFF audio, all the Dickheads listeners, and any one who takes the time to write reviews on Amazon or Goodreads.

David Agranoff is the award-nominated author of seven novels and two short story collections. His novels include *The Vegan Revolution...With Zombies, Punk Rock Ghost Story* and the Splatterpunk award nominated novel *Ring of Fire* from Deadite Press. His first short story collection *Screams from a Dying World* was nominated for the Wonderland award for best collection.

He is co-host of The Dickheads Podcast devoted to the work of Philip K Dick. www.soundcloud.com/dickheadspodcast. His blog has www.davidagranoff.blogspot.com has over 800 plus book reviews and updates on his books and podcasts. David grew-up in Bloomington Indiana but lives in San Diego with his wife and lots of rescued animals. Find him on social media: Twitter @DAgranoffauthor & Facebook: DAgranoffauthor so you can chat about Philip K. Dick, Horror movies, Vegan restaurants and his two basketball teams Indiana (in college) and the Portland Trailblazers.

GIMME THE LOOT: STORIES INSPIRED BY NOTORIOUS B.I.G

Edited by Gabino Iglesias

THE MISADVENTURES OF A JILTED JOURNALIST

Justin Little

NEW VERONIA

M.S. Coe

GODLESS HEATHENS: CONVERSATIONS WITH ATHEISTS

Edited by Andrew J. Rausch

DARK MOONS RISING IN A STARLESS NIGHT

Mame Bougouma Diene

NOHO GLOAMING & THE CURIOUS CODA OF ANTHONY SANTOS

Daniel Knauf (Creator of HBO's Carnivàle)

IF YOU DIED TOMORROW I WOULD EAT YOUR CORPSE

Wrath James White

THE ANACHIST KOSHER COOKBOOK

Maxwell Bauman

HORROR FILM POEMS

Poetry by Christoph Paul & Art by Joel Amat Güell

NIGHTMARES IN ECSTASY

Brendan Vidito

WE PUT THE LIT IN LITERARY

CL◀SH

CLASHBOOKS.COM